"The gas is called ZV," Phelps was saying into the phone. "An Army shipment was stolen in Utah during the early hours this morning. He's probably already been informed...Well, god damn it, I don't care if you don't know anything about it. He does...Yes, it's here..."

One of the men at the window said, "He must be insane."

"Of course," Graves said. "You'd have to be insane to wipe out a million people. But the fact is that we've really been lucky."

"Lucky?"

"Just see that he gets the message," Phelps said.

"Sure," Graves said. "Those Army shipments have been going on for years. They're sitting ducks. Anybody with a little money, a little intelligence, and a screw loose somewhere could arrange for a steal. Look: Richard Speck knocked off eight nurses, but he was an incompetent. Charles Whitman was an expert rifleman, and on that basis could knock off seventeen people. John Wright is highly intelligent and very wealthy. He's going to go for a million people and one American President. And thanks to the U.S. Army, he has a chance of succeeding..."

BINARY

by **Michael Crichton**

WRITING AS JOHN LANGE

A HARD CASE CRIME NOVEL

A HARD CASE CRIME BOOK
(HCC-MC8)
First Hard Case Crime edition: October 2013

Published by

Titan Books
A division of Titan Publishing Group Ltd
144 Southwark Street
London SE1 0UP

in collaboration with Winterfall LLC

BINARY™
by Michael Crichton writing as John Lange™

ISBN 978-1-78329-125-0

Design direction by Max Phillips
www.maxphillips.net

Typeset by Swordsmith Productions

The name "Hard Case Crime" and the Hard Case Crime logo are trademarks of Winterfall LLC. Hard Case Crime books are selected and edited by Charles Ardai.

Printed in the United States of America

Visit us on the web at www.HardCaseCrime.com

For
JASPER JOHNS
whose preoccupations
provided solutions

BINARY: any system composed of two interacting elements. As in binary stars, binary numbers, binary gases, etc.

Chemical agents lend themselves to covert use in sabotage against which it is exceedingly difficult to visualize any really effective defense...I will not dwell upon this use of CBW because, as one pursues the possibilities of such covert uses, one discovers that the scenarios resemble that in which the components of a nuclear weapon are smuggled into New York City and assembled in the basement of the Empire State Building.

In other words, once the possibility is recognized to exist, about all that one can do is worry about it.

—DR. IVAN L. BENNETT, JR.
TESTIFYING BEFORE THE SUBCOMMITTEE
ON NATIONAL SECURITY POLICY AND
SCIENTIFIC DEVELOPMENTS, NOVEMBER 20, 1969

This book was written before it became too embarrassing for the Republican party to hold its 1972 convention in San Diego, and I preferred not to follow the convention to Miami Beach.

—JOHN LANGE

BINARY

Prologue:
Beta Scenario

The facts are these:

1. On August 22, 1972, seven men flew into Salt Lake International Airport, Salt Lake City, Utah. The men came from Las Vegas, Chicago, Dallas, and New York. All seven men have been identified; they all have connections with organized crime. Thus far four have been picked up for questioning and their testimony provides the major portion of this report.

Each man was first contacted in his home city by an anonymous telephone call. They were each paid a thousand dollars in cash to do an unspecified job. All they knew in advance was that the job would take 48 hours, and that they must bring heavy boots and dark, warm clothing. Each was given an assumed name which he was to use for the duration of the job.

The men arrived in Salt Lake between noon and 4 P.M. local time. They were met separately. When all had arrived, they were transported in a 1968 white Plymouth sedan outside the city.

The trip out from Salt Lake was made in total silence. After an hour of travel they arrived in Ramrock, Utah, a town of 407 persons located in the north-central region of the state.

2. The men remained in Ramrock until nightfall, staying in a one-story wood frame house previously rented by an unknown party. While in the house, the seven men wore

surgical rubber gloves so that no fingerprints could be re-
covered. The men changed into their dark, heavy clothing
in the house, and received instructions on their job from the
leader, a man identified only as "Jones." Jones is described
as a heavyset muscular man with a broken nose and graying
hair. Positive identification has not yet been made of this
person.

3. Jones told the assembled men that they were going to steal
a quantity of insecticide from a train. He told them that he
had not personally planned the theft, that it had been worked
out by someone else. They believed this when they heard
the plans. Although not formally educated, these men have
a well-developed sense of personality and they all agree that
Jones, who was described by one as a "drill-sergeant type,"
lacked the acumen to formulate the plans.

4. The plans were remarkable for their detail. For example,
the men were told that the train would be traveling at 35 mph,
according to Department of Transportation regulations cov-
ering shipment of dangerous cargo. The men were told the
timetable the train would follow from its point of origin in
Dugway Proving Grounds, Utah, through the state. The men
were told of the existence of impedance trip sensors in the
rails, and were instructed in relay timing mechanisms involved.
They were told that the insecticide would be stored in 500-
pound canisters of two varieties—one kind painted yellow,
the other black. They were told that they must steal one
yellow canister and one black canister. Two yellows or two
blacks would not do.

Equally important is what the men were *not* told. They
were not told that the train would be guarded. This is an
important point. It means either that plans were drawn up
for the robbery one month before—when there were no

guards on the trains—or else that the presence of the guards was known by the planners, who elected not to inform the men. This point is still in debate.

The men were also not told why they were stealing the insecticide in the first place. Significantly, none of them asked. Apparently it was a matter of total indifference to them.

5. They remained in the wood frame house in Ramrock until 8 P.M. Then each man was issued a machine gun and a pistol. The machine guns were of the usual variety, that is, war surplus equipment sold with plugged barrels. Some other party had simply machined new barrels and replaced the original plugged barrels (cf. Memorandum 245/779: Abuses of War Surplus Weaponry). The men then climbed aboard a Land Rover which was stored in the garage of the house. It had apparently been there waiting for some weeks, because it was dusty. They drove off into the desert to meet the train.

6. They arrived at an unnamed site in northeast Utah shortly after 2 A.M. They carried out their preparations quickly and efficiently in the light of a full moon.

One man was sent down the tracks until he found the impedance trip sensor. He blocked the mechanism of this sensor by attaching an electronic override device. Thus no one knew for six hours that the train had been stopped further up the tracks; it was assumed that the trip sensor had broken down.

Meanwhile four other men walked across the sand toward a half-dozen cattle grazing nearby. The robbery site was minimal rangeland and had been chosen specifically because of this. The men shot the steer nearest to the tracks. The other cattle ran off at the sound of the shot.

The men looped ropes around the dead steer and dragged it across the railroad tracks. The animal was doused with gasoline and a timing device was attached to it.

Then all seven men climbed aboard the Land Rover and rode it to a nearby hiding place behind some low dunes. They waited approximately fifteen minutes before the train appeared in the distance. The men were surprised to see that it was a government train consisting of three flatcars lettered U.S. GOVERNMENT PROPERTY on the sides. They were also surprised to see an armored caboose at the end of the train.

7. The engine slowed, apparently as the engineer sighted the obstacle across the tracks. When the train stopped, the timing device caused the dead steer to burst into flames. At that moment six of the men ran forward, intending to remove the canisters. There was some scattered firing from the armored caboose. One man ran up to it, stuck his machine gun into an armored port, and delivered a burst of fire to the interior. All five soldiers (and one physician) inside the caboose were killed. The engineer was also killed a few moments later.

8. The men unloaded two canisters from the train, one black and one yellow. Each was marked with lettering so vivid that the men remembered it well; stenciled warnings to the effect that the canisters contained highly dangerous chemicals.

They carried the canisters across the desert to a flat location nearby. They set them down 100 yards apart and burned a red flare near each.

9. Two or three minutes passed, and then two helicopters appeared over the horizon. The helicopters landed in tandem alongside the flares. They were commercial helicopters of a nondescript nature. The only unusual aspect was that each had been fitted with a nylon web sling to hold a canister. The men loaded the canisters onto the slings. The helicopters lifted off again into the night.

10. The men returned to the Land Rover and drove back to Salt Lake City, arriving at 6 A.M. on the morning of August 23, 1972. Over the next 18 hours they flew out of the city to their points of origin. None had any knowledge of what happened to the canisters. None had any knowledge of the true contents of the canisters.

It is clear from the foregoing that these seven underworld figures were engaged in an activity closely approximating the RAND Corporation "Analog Scenario" sequence called CBW Beta. These scenarios were prepared in the fall of 1965 for the Department of Defense (Command and Control). They considered the options and ramifications of theft of thermonuclear bomb components and chem/biol agents.

Beta Scenario treated the possibility that a relatively small number of men, either criminal figures or political extremists, might steal these materials for blackmail, sabotage, or terrorist purposes The consequences of theft were considered uniformly disastrous. Therefore the scenario outlined ways to prevent this occurrence.

The chief preventive mechanism was deemed secrecy in transport schedules and methods. That is, the thieves would not know where, or when, the material was being shipped. As a result of the Beta Scenario conclusions, timetables for shipment were established by a closed-code computer mechanism operating from a table of random numbers. That mechanism was regarded as foolproof and unbreakable.

However, it is obvious that these seven men received instructions derived from breaking the timetable. It is not known how the timetable was broken, enabling the men to easily, almost effortlessly, steal one half-ton of the most potent nerve gas in the world.

Los Angeles: 5 a.m. PDT

Hour 12

The gray government sedan was waiting in a deserted corner of Los Angeles International Airport. Seen from the air, it cast a long shadow across the concrete runway in the pale morning light. He watched the sedan as his helicopter descended and landed a short distance from the car.

The driver came running up, bent over beneath the spinning blades, and opened the door. A gust of warm, dry August air swirled into the interior of the helicopter.

"Mr. Graves?"

"That's right."

"Come with me please."

Graves got out, carrying his briefcase, and walked to the car. He climbed into the back seat and they drove off away from the runway toward the freeway.

"Do you know where we're going?" Graves asked.

The driver consulted a clipboard. "One-oh-one-three-one-e Washington, Culver City, I have."

"I think that's right." Graves settled back in the seat. California numbering: he'd never get used to it. It was as bad as a zip code. He opened his early edition of *The New York Times* and tried to read it. He had tried on the helicopter but had found it impossible to concentrate. He assumed that was because of the noise. And the distractions: when they passed over San Clemente, halfway between Los Angeles and San Diego, he had been craning his neck, peering out the window like an ordinary tourist. The President was there now, had been for the last week.

He looked at the headlines: trouble in the UN, arguments in the German parliament about the mark, Britain and France squabbling...He put the paper aside and stared out the window at Los Angeles, flat and bleak in the early morning light.

"Good trip, sir?" the driver asked. It was perfectly said—no inflection, no prying, just detached polite interest. The driver didn't know who Graves was. He didn't know where he had come from. He didn't know what his business was. All the driver knew was that Graves was important enough to have a government helicopter fly him in and a government sedan pick him up.

"Fine, thanks." Graves smiled, staring out the window. In fact the trip had been horrible. Phelps had called him just an hour before and asked him to come up and give a briefing on Wright. That was the way Phelps worked—everything was a crisis, there were no routine activities. It was typical that Phelps hadn't bothered to let Graves know beforehand that he was even in Los Angeles.

Although on reflection, Graves knew he should have expected that. With the Republican Convention in San Diego, all the activity of the country had shifted from Washington to the West Coast. The President was in the Western White House in San Clemente; the Convention was 80 miles to the south; and Phelps—what would Phelps do? Obviously, relocate discreetly in the nearest large city, which was Los Angeles. As Graves considered it, Los Angeles became the inevitable choice.

Phelps needed the telephone lines for data transmission. It was as simple as that. L.A. was the third largest city in America, and it would have plenty of telephone lines that the Department of State (Intelligence Division) could take over on short notice. It was inevitable.

"Here we are, sir," the driver said, pulling over to the curb. He got out and opened the door for Graves. "Am I to wait for you, sir?"

"Yes, I think so."

"Very good, sir."

Graves paused and looked up at the building. It was a rather ordinary four-story office building in an area of Los Angeles that seemed almost a slum. The building, not particularly new, was outstandingly ugly. And the paint was flaking away from the facade.

Graves walked up the steps and entered the lobby. As he went through the doors he looked at his watch. It was exactly 5 A.M. Phelps was waiting for him in the deserted lobby. Phelps wore a lightweight glen-plaid suit and a worried expression. He shook hands with Graves and said, "How was your flight?" His voice echoed slightly in the lobby.

"Fine," Graves said.

They walked to the elevators, passing the ground-floor offices, which seemed mostly devoted to a bank.

"Like this place?" Phelps said.

"Not much."

"It was the best we could find on short notice," he said.

A guard with a sign-in book stood in front of the elevators. Graves let Phelps sign first; then he took the pen and wrote his name, his authorization, and the time. He saw that Decker and Venn were already there.

They got onto the elevator and pressed the button for the third floor. "Decker and Venn are already here," Phelps said.

"I saw."

Phelps nodded and smiled, as much as he ever smiled. "I keep forgetting about you and your powers of observation."

"I keep forgetting about you, too," Graves said.

Phelps ignored the remark. "I've planned two meetings for today," he said. "You've got the briefing in an hour—Wilson, Peckham, and a couple of others. But I think you should hear about Sigma Station first."

"All right," Graves said. He didn't know what the hell Phelps was talking about, but he wasn't going to give him the satisfaction of asking.

They got off at the third floor and walked past some peeling posters of Milan and Tahiti and through a small typing pool, the desks now deserted, the typewriters neatly covered.

"What is this place?" Graves said.

"Travel agency," Phelps said. "They went out of business but they had a lot of—"

"Telephone lines."

"Yes. We took over the floor."

"How long you planning to stay?" Graves asked. There was an edge to his voice that he didn't bother to conceal. Phelps knew how he felt about the Department.

"Just through the Convention," Phelps said, with elaborate innocence. "What did you think?"

"I thought it might be permanent."

"Good Lord, no. Why would we do a thing like that?"

"I can't imagine," Graves said.

Past the typing pool they came to a section of private offices. The walls were painted an institutional beige. It reminded Graves of a prison, or a hospital. No wonder the travel agency went out of business, he thought.

"I know how you feel," Phelps said.

"Do you?" Graves asked.

"Yes. You're…ambivalent about the section."

"I'm ambivalent about the domestic activities."

"We all are," Phelps said. He said it easily, in the smooth, oil-on-the-waters manner that he had perfected. And his father before him. Phelps's father had been an undersecretary of state during the Roosevelt administration. Phelps himself was a product of the Dalton School, Andover, Yale, and Harvard Law School. If he sat still, ivy would sprout from his ears. But he never sat still.

"How do you find San Diego?" he asked, walking along with his maddeningly springy step.

"Boring and hot."

Phelps sighed. "Don't blame me. *I* didn't choose it."

Graves did not reply. They continued down a corridor and came upon a guard, who nodded to Phelps. "Good morning, Mr. Phelps." And to Graves: "Good morning, sir." Phelps flashed his pink card; so did Graves. The guard allowed them to pass further down the corridor past a large banner that read FIRST CLASS SERVICE ON COACH.

"You've got a guard already," Graves said.

"There's a lot of expensive equipment to look after," Phelps said. They made a right turn and entered a conference room.

There were just four of them: Graves; Phelps, looking springy and alert as he greeted everyone; Decker, who was thin and dark, intense-looking; and Venn, who was nearly fifty, graying, sloppy in his dress. Graves had never met Decker or Venn before, but he knew they were both scientists. They were too academic and too uncomfortable to be anything else.

Phelps ran the meeting. "This is John Graves, who is the world's foremost expert on John Wright." He smiled slightly. "Mr. Graves has plenty of background, so you can speak as technically as you want. Decker, why don't you begin."

Decker cleared his throat and opened a briefcase in front of him, removing a sheaf of computer printout. He slipped through the green pages as he spoke. "I've been working in Special Projects Division for the last six months," he said. "I was assigned to establish redundancy programs on certain limited-access files so that we could check call-up locations to these data banks, which are mostly located in Arlington Hall in Washington."

He paused and glanced at Graves to see if the information was making sense. Graves nodded.

"The problem is basically one of access-line proliferation. A data bank is just a collection of information stored on magnetic tape drums. It can be anywhere in the country. To get information out of it, you need to hook into the main computer with an access substation. That can also be anywhere in the country. Every major data bank has a large number of access substations. For limited or special-purpose access—stations that need to draw out information once or twice a week, let's say—we employ commercial telephone lines; we don't have our own lines. To tie in to a peripheral computer substation, you telephone a call number and hook your phone up to the computer terminal. That's it. As long as you have a half-duplex or full-duplex telephone line, you're in business."

Graves nodded. "How is the call number coded?"

"We'll come to that," Decker said, looking at Venn. "For now, we'll concentrate on the system. Some of the major data banks, like the ones held by Defense, may have five hundred or a thousand access lines. A year ago, Wilkens's congressional committee started to worry about unauthorized tapping into those access lines. In theory, a bright boy who knew computers could tap into the system and call out any information he wanted from the data banks. He could get all sorts of classified information."

Decker sighed. "So I was hired to install redundancy checks on the system. Echo checks, bit additions, that sort of thing. My job was to make sure we could verify which stations drew out information from the data banks, and what information they drew. I finished that work a month ago."

Graves glanced at Phelps. Phelps was watching them all intently, pretending he was following the discussion. Graves knew that it was over Phelps's head.

"Just before I finished," Decker said, "we discovered that an unauthorized station was tapping into the system. We called it Sigma Station, but we were unable to characterize it. By that I mean that we knew Sigma was drawing information, but we didn't know where, or how."

He flipped to a green sheet of computer printout and pushed it across the table to Graves. "Sigma is the under-lined station. You can see that on this particular day, July 21, 1972, it tapped into the system at ten oh four p.m. Eastern time and maintained the contact for seven minutes; then it broke out. We determined that Sigma was tapping in at around ten o'clock two or three nights a week. But that was all we knew."

Decker turned to Venn, who said, "I came into the picture at this point. I'd been at Bell Labs working on telephone tracer mechanisms. The telephone company has a problem with unauthorized calls—calls verbally charged to a phony number, calls charged to a wrong credit card number, that kind of thing. I was working on a computer tracing system. Defense asked me to look at the Sigma Station problem."

"One ought to say," Phelps said, "that the data bank being tapped by Sigma was a Defense bank."

"Yes," Venn said. "It was a Defense bank. With two or three taps a week at about ten p.m. That was all I knew when I began. However, I made some simple assumptions. First, you've got to have a computer terminal in order to tap the system. That is, once you've called the number that links you to the computer, you must use a teletype-writing or CRT apparatus compatible with the Defense system."

"Are those terminals common?"

"No," Venn said. "They are quite advanced and fairly uncommon. I started with a list of them."

Graves nodded.

"Then I considered the timing. Ten p.m. Eastern time is seven p.m. in California, where most of these sophisticated terminals in defense industry applications are located. If an employee were illegally using a terminal to tap into Defense, he couldn't do it during office hours. On the other hand, it requires an extraordinary access to get into an East Coast terminal location at ten at night—or into a Midwest location at eight or nine. Therefore Sigma was probably on the West Coast."

"So you checked the West Coast terminals?"

"Yes. Because in order to hook into the Defense system, you'd have to unhook from your existing system. What corporation, R&D group, or production unit had a terminal that was unhooked at seven p.m. Western time twice a week? Answer: None. New question: What group had its terminals repaired twice a week? Repairing would entail unhooking. Answer: the Southern California Association of Insurance Underwriters, a company based in San Diego."

Graves said, "So you investigated the repairman and you found—"

"We found our man," Venn said, looking slightly annoyed with Graves. "His name is Timothy Drew. He has been doing repair work on the S.C. Association computers for about six weeks. It turns out nobody authorized those repairs; he just showed up and—"

"But you haven't picked him up."

Phelps coughed. "No, actually. We haven't picked him up yet because he's—"

"Disappeared," Graves said.

"That's right," Phelps said. "How did you know?"

"Tim Drew is a friend of John Wright. He's had dinner with him several times a week for the last month or so." As he spoke, Graves had a mental image of Drew—early thirties, blond-looking, muscular. Graves had run a check on him some weeks back and had discovered only that Drew was an ex-Army lieutenant, discharged one year before. A clean record in computer work, nothing good, nothing bad.

"We weren't able to find him," Venn said, "but we're still looking. We thought—"

Graves said, "There's only one thing I want to know. What information did Drew tap from the classified files?"

There was a long silence around the table. Finally Decker said, "We don't know."

"You don't know?" Graves lit a cigarette. "But that's the most important question—"

"Let me explain," Decker said. "Drew was an ex-Army officer with knowledge of computer systems. He knew that he couldn't call in on any old number. The call-in numbers are changed at irregular intervals, roughly once a week. But the possible permutations of the call-in number aren't great. With trial and error, he might have found it."

"You know he found the number," Graves said, "because you know he tapped in. The question is, what did he tap *out* from the system?"

"Well, once he was hooked up, he still had a problem. You

need subroutine codes to extract various kinds of information, and—"

"How often are the codes changed?"

"Not very often."

Graves found himself getting impatient. "How often are the codes changed?"

"About once a year."

Graves sighed. "So Drew might have used his old codes to get what he wanted?"

"Yes."

"Then we want to know what codes he knew. What sort of work did Drew do when he was in the Army?"

"He did topological work. Surface configurations, shipment routings, that sort of thing."

Graves glanced at Phelps. "Can we be more specific?"

"I'm afraid not," Phelps said. "Defense is unwilling to release Drew's work record to us. Defense is a little defensive, you might say, about the fact that this tap occurred in the first place."

There was a long silence. Graves stared at the men around the table. There were times, he thought, when working for the government was an exercise in total stupidity. Finally he said, "How can you get Defense to release the information?"

"I'm not sure we can," Phelps said. "But one of the reasons you're being briefed is that we were hoping you might be able to shed light on the situation."

"I might?"

"Yes. Drew was working for Wright, after all."

Before Graves could answer, the telephone rang. Phelps answered it, and said, "Yes, thank you," and hung up. He looked at Graves. "Do you have any thoughts about this?"

"None," Graves said.

"None at all?"

"None at all."

"Well," Phelps said, "perhaps something will occur to you in the next hour." He gave Graves a heavily disapproving look, then stood up and turned to Decker and Venn. "Thank you, gentlemen," he said. And to Graves: "Let's go."

Los Angeles: 6 a.m. PDT

Hour 11

Another conference room, another group. This room was decorated entirely in Tahiti posters; it occurred to Graves that whoever had owned the travel agency before it went bankrupt was a Tahiti-nut. Perhaps he was himself Tahitian. Graves began to wonder why the Tahitian owner had gone out of business. Too much time away from the office, basking in the sun? Discrimination against him by Angelenos? Some rare disease carried by coconuts which had made him an invalid?

"Gentlemen," Phelps said, and cleared his throat. Graves was snapped back to the present. He looked around the room. There were, he saw, a number of high-ranking Washington people. They all looked tired and disgruntled. Phelps had brought them out to California on a red-eye flight, let them sleep a few hours, then dragged them up for a meeting with... John Graves?

"John Graves," Phelps said, "has come up from San Diego this morning to brief you on John Wright. Mr. Graves has been in charge of Wright's surveillance in New York and San Diego for the past three months." Phelps nodded to Graves, and Graves stood.

"We have some footage which is quite revealing," Graves said. "I thought we'd begin with that, if we can screen it..."

The men in the room looked confused. Even Phelps, who never lost his aplomb, seemed uncertain. Graves settled it by tearing down several Tahitian posters from the wall, clearing a blank white space. He was embarrassed for a moment—

the tearing noise sounded somehow indiscreet with all these Washington guns, and the whole business emphasized the makeshift nature of the surroundings.

Phelps seemed to sense it, too. "You must excuse us," he said, "but these are temporary quarters for the duration of the Republican Convention."

Graves stepped to one side as the room lights dimmed. A black-and-white image was projected on the wall. It showed a dapper, rather handsome man standing at a podium. For a moment there was no sound, and then it came on abruptly. The voice was sharp, vigorous, and slightly petulant.

"—can a person do in the twentieth century? The question is not rhetorical, my friends. Each and every one of us is powerless in the face of giant corporations, giant institutions, giant government Do you think automobiles are badly made? Do you think your electricity bill is too high? Do you disagree with the nation's foreign policy? Well, there's nothing much you can do about it. No matter what you think, or I think, the wheels continue to spin of their own inertia."

The film image of John Wright paused to take a drink of water. "Perhaps you think that a few people have power— high government officials, high corporate executives, wealthy individuals. But that also is untrue. Everyone is locked into a system which he has inherited and is powerless to change. We are all trapped, my friends. That is the meaning of the twentieth century. It is the century of impotence."

Wright's voice dropped lower, became more ominous. His face was grim. "Impotence," he repeated. "Inability to act. Inability to be effective. This is what we must change. And with the help of God, we shall."

There was some applause on the soundtrack before the film ran out of the camera and the room lights came back on. Graves lit a cigarette and flipped through the pages of his own file on Wright before speaking.

"I showed you that film for psychological, not political, reasons," he said, "because it summarizes most of what we know about John Wright's mental state. The speech was given last year before the annual conference of the Americans for a Better Nation, an extremist group which Wright started and still leads. You've probably never heard of it. It's small, and has no significance whatsoever in national politics. Over the last few years, Wright has poured 1.7 million dollars into the organization. The money apparently doesn't matter to him. But the lack of impact—the impotence—matters a great deal."

He paused and glanced around the faces at the table. They seemed to be paying attention, but just barely. Two were doodling on the pads before them. "John Wright," he said, "is now forty-nine years old. He is the son of Edmund Wright, of the Wright steel family. He is an only child. His father was a crude, domineering man and an alcoholic. John grew up in his shadow, a very strange child. He was a good student and learned quite a lot of mathematics, even made a minor reputation for himself in that field. On the other hand, he was an inveterate gambler, horse racer, and womanizer."

The assembled men began to fidget. Graves nodded to the projectionist, who began flashing up slides. The first showed Edmund Wright glaring into the camera. "Edmund Wright died of cirrhosis in 1955. John Wright changed completely when that happened. He moved to New York from Pittsburgh and became a kind of local celebrity. He was married four times to well-known actresses; all the marriages ended in divorce. The last divorce, from Sarah Layne, occurred in 1967 and coincided with a six-month nervous breakdown for Wright.

He was hospitalized in McClain General outside Atlanta for paranoid ideation and feelings of impotence. Apparently he had been impotent with his last wife."

A picture of Sarah Layne flashed up. The men all stirred uncomfortably as they stared at the image: handsome, but haughty and undeniably challenging.

"Wright left the hospital against doctor's advice and plunged into the political organization he formed: Americans for a Better Nation. For the next four years he gave speeches and wrote pamphlets. In 1968 he worked hard to influence the national elections on every level—mostly without success. He fell into a depression after that.

"Recently, his interest in politics dropped sharply. He seems to have withdrawn from any kind of public life; he no longer holds large parties and no longer participates in the social life of New York. According to all information, he has been intensely studying a variety of subjects that are rather ominous. These include sociology, radiation theory, physics, and some aspects of biology. He has interviewed experts in several different areas—" Graves flipped the pages of his file "—including cancer experts, civil engineers, horticulture specialists, and aerosol spray-can designers. He—"

"Aerosol spray-can designers?" someone asked.

"That is correct."

There was some head scratching among those present.

"He also became interested in the meteorology of the Southwest."

The men were listening now and looking very puzzled. All the doodling had stopped.

"Wright was listed as a Potential Surveillance Subject at the end of 1968, after he had engaged in some questionable activities to influence the national election. As a PSS he did nothing out of the ordinary until six months ago. Then two things happened.

"First, Wright began to transfer large amounts of money from various accounts in this country and in Switzerland. As you know, we keep an eye on private capital transfers in excess of $300,000. Wright was moving much more than that. Secondly, he began to be seen with known underworld figures. The pattern of behavior suggested a courtship, and we became very concerned at that point."

The slides changed again several times in rapid succession, showing smooth-faced businessmen. "Robert 'Trigger' Canino. Sal Martucci. Benny Flick. Gerald 'Tiny' Margolin. These are some of the men he saw during that period."

The slides now showed Wright in restaurants, at taxi stands, and in Central Park with these men.

"Active surveillance began in June 1972, when Wright left New York for San Diego. He was clearly making plans for the Republican Convention, but their nature was not clear, and he was giving himself much too much time. I ran the surveillance from the start. During the surveillance period his contacts with organized crime have substantially decreased. He has been seeing only one person consistently—this man."

The screen showed a bald, glowering face.

"Eddie 'The Key' Trasker, fifty-three, a resident of Las Vegas who lives mostly in San Diego. He is reputed to be the power behind the Teamsters, and his influence over all forms of interstate transportation is enormous. Wright has seen him nearly every week, often during the early hours of the morning.

"He has also come in contact with this man, Timothy Drew, an ex-Army officer with a background in computers.

The meaning of that association was unclear to me until this morning. Drew clearly represents Sigma Station; Drew tapped out classified Defense information for Wright. We do not know what kind of information, or why it was stolen."

Graves sat down and looked at the faces. Phelps said, "Questions, gentlemen?"

McPherson, from the President's staff, cleared his throat. "I gather from Mr. Graves's excellent but rather psycho-logically oriented presentation that we have no damned idea what Wright is up to. Is that substantially correct?"

"Yes, it is," Graves said.

"Well then," McPherson said, "I'm afraid we can do nothing. Wright has acted suspiciously and is quite probably deranged. Neither is a crime in this country."

"I disagree," Corey said, sitting back in his chair. Corey was Defense liaison; a heavyset man with thick eyebrows that joined over his nose. "I think we have plenty of reason to apprehend Wright at this time."

"Plenty of reason," McPherson said, "but no evidence, no charges…"

Whitlock, from the Justice Department, straightened his tie and said, "I'm sure we all agree this is an unpleasant sort of meeting. Mr. Wright is a private citizen and he is entitled to do as he pleases so long as he does not commit a crime. I've seen and heard nothing that suggests a crime has been or will be committed, and—"

"What about the underworld contacts?" Corey said.

Whitlock smiled. "What about them?"

"I think that's very suggestive—"

"But he has broken no law," Whitlock said. "And until he does…" He shrugged.

Corey frowned, pushing his eyebrows into a black, ominous V. "An interrogation would be useful, even without a criminal act," he said. "I think we have a basis for interrogation here —Wright's association with Timothy Drew, who has stolen classified information, probably for Wright. Can't we pick him up on that?"

"I feel we should," Phelps said, speaking for the first time.

Graves spun around to look at Phelps.

"I disagree," McPherson said.

Whitlock made some notes on the pad in front of him. Finally he said, "Perhaps an interrogation is the safest route. I think we need to know what was tapped out by Sigma Station. Mr. Corey?"

"Pick him up."

"Mr. Phelps?"

"Pick him up."

"Mr. McPherson?"

"Opposed."

Whitlock spread his hands. Graves said nothing. The meeting was over.

"If there are no further questions," Phelps said, "we can adjourn."

"You didn't like that, did you?" Phelps said, as they walked back through the travel agency.

"No," Graves said. "I didn't."

"Still," Phelps said, "I think it's best. Arrest him today, on suspicion of conspiracy to commit grand larceny involving classified information."

"Isn't it robbery?"

Phelps sighed patiently. "Robbery and larceny are different crimes."

Graves said, "How long can I wait?"

"A few hours. Play with him if you want, but pick him up by evening. I want to get to the bottom of this."

Graves couldn't make the arrest himself. He'd need federal marshals. "You'll notify the marshals in San Diego?"

"They're waiting for your call," Phelps said, and smiled. As much as he ever did.

Graves had fifteen minutes before he had to return to the airport. As he walked out of the travel agency, he heard a room filled with mechanical chatter. Curious, he paused and opened the door. He found that one office had been converted into a temporary hardware room. It had once been somebody's office, but now there were six teletypes and computer consoles installed there. He was reminded that the State Department (Intelligence Division) and the NSA had more computers than any other organizations in the world.

The room was empty at this hour. He glanced at the teletypes, noting their color. When he first started working at State in the early sixties, rooms like this had contained five red teletypes and one blue teletype. The red machines recorded information from overseas stations and embassies; the blue was for domestic data. Now, four of the machines were blue and only two were red.

There had been a shift in orientation for State Intelligence. Nobody cared any longer about the movements of an eighth assistant deputy minister in the Yugoslav government. They were much more interested in the number five man in the Black Panther Party, or the number three man in the John Birch Society, or the number six man in Americans for a Better Nation.

He sat down at a computer console, stared at the blank TV screen, and began typing in Wright's call numbers. The screen glowed and printed out the categories of stored information:

WRIGHT, JOHN HENSEN
001 FILE SUMMARY
002 PERSONAL APPEARANCE, COMPLETE
003 PHOTOS
004 PERSONAL HISTORY, COMPLETE
005 RECENT ACTIVITIES (2 WEEK UPDATE)
006 FINANCIAL HISTORY, COMPLETE
007 POLITICAL HISTORY, COMPLETE
008 MISCELLANEOUS
009 CROSS REFERENCES LISTING, COMPLETE

Graves stared at the categories with some distaste. It was disturbing that the government should have so much information on a private individual—particularly one who had committed no criminal act at any time.

Then on an impulse he pushed the "Wipe" button and the screen went blank. He typed in "Graves, John Norman," followed by his own call-up number. He sat back and watched the numbers print out on the screen:

GRAVES, JOHN NORMAN 445798054
INTELLIGENCE, DEPT STATE/INVESTIGATIONS
(DOM)
TELEPHONE: 808-415-7800 X 4305
FILE CONTENTS CANNOT BE DISPLAYED ON THIS
CONSOLE WITHOUT AUTHORIZATION VQ.

He hesitated, then punched "Auth: VQ"

AUTHORIZATION VQ RECORDED
STATE NAME

After another hesitation, he punched "Phelps, Richard D."

RECORD CALL-UP NAME AS PHELPS, RICHARD D.

FILE CONTENTS CANNOT BE DISPLAYED ON THIS
CONSOLE TO THE ABOVENAMED PERSON. CALL-
UP PERSON IS ADVISED TO ACQUIRE NTK
AUTHORIZATION FROM DEPARTMENT HEAD.

Graves smiled. So even Phelps couldn't call up Graves's file
without a special need-to-know authorization. Who *could*
call it up? Feeling whimsical, he typed out "This is the
President of the United States."

The screen glowed:

RECORD CALL-UP AS
PRESIDENTOFTHEUNITEDSTATES
IS THIS A CODE NAME
STATE GIVEN NAME

Graves sighed. Computers just didn't show any respect. He
pressed the "Wipe" button and returned to the question of
Wright.

He didn't really know what he was looking for. Graves
had supplied most of the computerized file contents himself.
But perhaps someone else had added to it He pushed the 008
sequence calling up miscellaneous information. That cate-
gory had been empty two weeks ago. Now it contained an
academic history of Wright's work in mathematics, prepared
by "S. Vessen, State/Anal/412." Whoever that was. He had a
moment of pleasure at the thought that State's analysis people
were abbreviated "anal." It was fitting.

He turned to the information itself:

HX ACADEMIC—JOHN WRIGHT (BIBLIO FOLLOWS:
008/02)

WRIGHT STUDIED MATHEMATICS AT PRINCETON
UNDER REIMANN. FROM THE START HIS INTEREST,

LIKE THAT OF HIS TEACHER, WAS HEAVILY STATISTICAL AND PROBABILISTIC. HIS FIRST PAPER CONCERNED STOCK MARKET FLUCTUATIONS. THIS WAS WRITTEN IN 1942, BEFORE HIGH SPEED DIGITAL COMPUTERS WERE AVAILABLE. HOWEVER, WITHOUT SUCH TOOLS WRIGHT DECIDED THAT THE STOCK MARKET WAS TOTALLY RANDOM IN ITS BEHAVIOR. (THAT IS, THE CHANCE THAT A GIVEN STOCK WOULD GO UP OR DOWN ON ANY DAY BORE NO RELATIONSHIP TO WHAT IT HAD DONE THE PREVIOUS DAY.) THIS FACT WAS FINALLY CONFIRMED BEYOND ALL DOUBT IN 1961.

WRIGHT WAS ALSO INTERESTED IN SPORTS AND GAMBLING. IN 1944 HE WROTE AN AMUSING SHORT ARTICLE "ON BEING DUE." IN IT HE ARGUED CORRECTLY THAT THE ORDINARY NOTION THAT A MAN IS "DUE FOR A HIT" IF HE HAS BEEN RECENTLY UNSUCCESSFUL AT BAT IS TOTALLY FALLACIOUS. EACH TIME AT BAT IS A SEPARATE EVENT.

HE WAS ALSO INTERESTED IN HISTORICAL CONTEXTS: THE FACT THAT JOHN ADAMS, JAMES MONROE, AND THOMAS JEFFERSON ALL DIED ON JULY 4, AND SO ON. HE WROTE A PAPER ON ASSIGNING CAUSATION TO HISTORICAL AND POLITICAL EVENTS. IN THIS WORK HE WAS STRONGLY INFLUENCED BY THEORETICAL PHYSICISTS.

HE SHOWED THAT YOU CAN NEVER DETERMINE "THE CHIEF REASON" FOR THE AMERICAN CIVIL WAR, NAPOLEON'S DEFEAT AT WATERLOO, THE

FALL OF THE ROMAN EMPIRE, OR ANY OTHER
HISTORICAL EVENT. THE CHIEF REASON CANNOT
BE KNOWN IN ANY PRECISE SENSE. FOR ANY
EVENT THERE ARE HUNDREDS OR THOUSANDS
OF CONTRIBUTING CAUSES, AND NO WAY TO
ASSIGN PRIORITIES TO THESE CAUSES.
HISTORIANS HAVE ATTACKED THE WRIGHT
THESIS VIGOROUSLY SINCE IT TENDS TO PUT
THEM OUT OF A JOB. HE WAS, HOWEVER,
MATHEMATICALLY CORRECT BEYOND DOUBT.

FINALLY WRIGHT TURNED TO THE GENERAL
THEORY OF INTERACTIONS. FOR SIMPLICITY HE
STUDIED TWO-COMPONENT INTERACTIONS
LEADING TO A SINGLE EVENT OR OUTCOME. HE
BECAME QUITE KNOWLEDGEABLE IN THIS AREA.

SUMMARY:
WRIGHT IS A TALENTED MATHEMATICIAN
WHOSE PERSONAL INTERESTS FALL IN THE
AREA OF PROBABILITY AND STATISTICS AS
THEY APPLY TO HUMAN ACTIVITIES SUCH AS
SPORTS, GAMBLING, AND THE INTERPRETATION
OF HISTORY. HIS DEVELOPMENT AS A
MATHEMATICIAN DISPOSED HIM TO BE
INTERESTED IN TWO-COMPONENT
INTERACTIONS LEADING TO A SINGLE
EVENT OR OUTCOME.

Graves stared at the screen. The notion of two-component
interactions fascinated him. It seemed to have all sorts of
connotations. He punched buttons and looked at the bibli-
ography, which was not revealing. He looked at the abstracts
of articles written by Wright. They were equally unrevealing.

Then he saw that a final study was available: Apparently
S. Vessen had applied a statistical analysis of his own to
Wright's work.

S. VESSEN: ANALYSIS OF WORD FREQUENCIES IN
PAPERS OF JOHN WRIGHT.
THE FOLLOWING WORDS APPEAR MORE
FREQUENTLY THAN EXPECTED ACCORDING TO
RATIOS OF TOTAL WORDAGE FOR MATHEMATICAL
TREATISES

PROBABILITY
COINCIDENCE
GAUSSIAN
INSTABILITY
INTERACTION
TWO-COMPONENT
IMPOTENCE

Graves frowned, staring at the last word. Then he pressed the
"Wipe" button a final time and hurried to catch his plane.

En Route to San Diego: 7 a.m. PDT

Hour 10

The aircraft banked steeply over the oil fields of Long Beach and headed south toward San Diego. Graves stared out the window, thinking of Wright's file. Then he thought about his own. He wondered what it looked like, the information displayed on the unblinking cathode-ray screen in sharp white easy-to-read block letters. He wondered how accurate it was, how fair, how honest, how kind.

Graves was thirty-six years old. He had worked for the government fifteen years—nearly half his life. That fact implied a dedication which had never been there; from the start his career in government had been a kind of accident.

In college Graves had studied subjects that interested him, whether they were practical or not. On the surface they seemed highly impractical: Russian literature and mathematics. He was drafted immediately after college and did push-ups for five weeks before somebody in the Army discovered what he knew. Then he was sent to the language school in Monterey, where he remained forty-eight hours— just long enough to be tested—before being flown to Washington.

That was in 1957, and the Cold War was grim. Washington needed Russian translators desperately. There were fears of a land war in Europe, fears of grand conquistadorial campaigns conducted by World Communism, meaning those two friendly allies, Russia and China. At the time the fears had seemed compelling and logical.

Graves worked for two years in the Army as a Slavic

translator, and after his discharge joined the State Department in the same capacity. The pay was good and the work was interesting; he had the feeling of being useful, of doing necessary and even important work. In 1959 he married a girl on Senator Westlake's staff. They had a daughter in 1961. They got divorced two years later. He had a kidney stone and spent five days in the hospital. He met a nice girl, almost married her, but didn't. He bought a new car. He moved to a new apartment.

In retrospect, these seemed to be the signposts, the significant shifts and alterations in his life. The years went by: he wore his hair a little longer, but the hair was thinner, exposing more of his temples. His trousers got tight, then flared, and now were baggy again, as they had been in the fifties. There were cyclic changes in himself and his world—but he was still working for the government.

State no longer wanted Russian translators. The big push was for Chinese and Japanese translators. Graves transferred into Intelligence, a division of State that was highly mathematical, heavily computerized. He worked in the foreign division for five years, doing a lot of code breaking. At that time the foreign embassies were all utilizing computer-generated codes of various kinds, and it was challenging work—even if the messages usually turned out to be requests for funds to refurbish the ballroom on the second floor, or to hire additional kitchen help. Graves was interested in the codes, not in the content.

In 1970 he was moved to the domestic end. It seemed a minor change at the time, and a change he welcomed. He was ready to do something different. It was a long time before he realized just how different it was.

During his fifteen years in the government, slowly and

imperceptibly his enemy had shifted from the Big Bear, the Russkies, the Reds, the ChiComs—to his fellow Americans. That was his job now, and he hated it. It was tapping telephone transmissions and competing with other agencies; it was value judgments and it was very, very political.

Nothing was clean and direct anymore. And Graves didn't like it. Not anymore.

Graves had been planning to quit State for a long time, ever since his domestic work had become distasteful. But he hadn't quit.

What kept him was partly inertia and partly the fear that he might be unable to teach Slavic or mathematics. At least, that was what he told himself. He was reluctant to admit the real reason, even to himself.

The fact was that he took a genuine pleasure in his work. The pleasure was abstract, the pleasure of a compulsive jigsaw puzzle worker who will fit the pieces together without caring what the puzzle really means. It was a game he loved to play, even if it was fundamentally nasty.

He also liked the notion of an opponent. In the foreign division he had been up against institutions—embassies, foreign press corps, political groups of various kinds. In the domestic division, it was most often a single individual.

Graves had long ago discovered his skill at poker, backgammon, and chess—games which required a combination of mathematical insight, memory, and psychological daring. To him the ideal was chess—one man pitted against another man, each trying to calculate the intentions of the other in a game of enormous complexity with many alternatives.

That was why he had agreed to leave Washington in order to follow the activities of John Wright. In the realm of puzzles and games, nothing was more challenging than John Wright.

He and Wright were well matched: the same intelligence, the same mathematical background, the same fondness for games, particularly chess and poker.

But now after three months, Phelps was rolling him up. Wright would be arrested; the game would be called off. Graves sighed, trying to tell himself that this did not represent a personal defeat. Yet it was; he knew it.

With a low whine the plane began its descent toward San Diego, skimming in over the roofs of the highest buildings. Graves didn't much like San Diego. It was a utilitarian town dominated by the needs of the Navy, which ran it with a firm, conservative hand. Even its sins were dreary: the downtown area was filled with bars, pool halls, and porno movie houses which advertised "Beaver films—direct from Frisco!" as if San Francisco were six thousand miles away and not just an hour up the coast. Fresh-faced sailors wandered all over the downtown area looking for something to do. They never seemed to understand that there was nothing to do. Except, possibly, to get drunk.

Despite the early hour San Diego was hot, and Graves was grateful for the car's air conditioning. Lewis drove away from the airport, glancing occasionally at Graves. "The marshals checked in with us an hour ago."

"So you know?"

"Everybody knows. They're just waiting for you to say the word."

As they left the airport they passed beneath a banner stretched across the road: WELCOME REPUBLICANS. Graves smiled. "I'm going to hold off for a while," he said. "At least until this afternoon."

Lewis nodded and said nothing. Graves liked that about him, his silence. He was young and enthusiastic—characteristics Graves severely lacked—but he knew when to keep his mouth shut. "We'll go directly to his apartment," he said.

"All right," Lewis said. He didn't ask why.

"What time did Wright quit last night?"

"Nine. Lights out at nine."

"Rather early." Graves frowned. It was rare for Wright to go to bed before midnight.

"Duly noted on the time-clock sheets," Lewis said. "I checked them myself this morning."

"Has he ever done that before? Gone to bed at nine?"

"July fifth. He had the flu then, you remember."

"But he's not sick now," Graves said, and tugged at his ear. It was a nervous habit he had. And he was very nervous now.

There were a lot of cops stationed on the road from the airport to the city. Graves commented on it.

"You haven't heard?" Lewis said.

"Heard what?"

"The President's coming in today."

"No," Graves said. "When was that decided? This is only the second day. I'm surprised he'd show before he's nominated."

"Everybody's surprised. Apparently he intends to address the Convention delegates before the balloting."

"Oh?"

"Yeah." Lewis smiled. "It's also apparently true that there are some squabbles in the rules committee and the platform committee. He's going to straighten that out."

"Ah." It was making more sense. The President was a practical politician. He'd sacrifice the drama of a grand entrance if he had to get a political job done earlier.

"We just got the word a couple of hours ago," Lewis said. "Same with the police. They're furious. The Chief has been making statements about how hard it is to provide security…" He gestured at all the waiting cops. They were stationed every 30 yards or so along the road. "I guess he managed."

"Looks like it. What time is he due?"

"Around noon, I think."

They drove on in silence for a while, leaving the coast road and heading into the center of town. Graves noticed that Broadway had been dressed up, its honky-tonk glitter subdued a little. But there were a lot of tough-looking girls around.

Lewis commented on it. "The City Fathers are going crazy," he said. "About *that*." He jerked his thumb toward one spectacularly constructed girl in a tightly clinging pants suit.

"I thought it wasn't allowed." Traditionally San Diego was free of hookers despite the large sailor population. Tijuana was just 20 minutes away; those services were usually provided across the border.

"Nothing they can do about it," Lewis said. "Just in the last few hours they've all been coming in. Every damned hooker for a thousand miles is here. All the girls from Vegas and Reno and Tahoe. It's the Convention."

"But the City Fathers don't like it."

"The City Fathers hate it," Lewis said, and grinned. It was a youthful grin, the grin of a person who still found sin amusing, risqué fun.

Graves could no longer find the fun in prostitution. Why not? he wondered. Was it age—or was it striking some uncomfortable chord in himself?

But he didn't pursue the thought. Lewis turned left, going up into the hilly section of town toward Wright's apartment.

San Diego: 8 a.m. PDT
Hour 9

Lewis slowed as they approached a dry cleaning van advertising 24 HOUR SERVICE AT NO ADDITIONAL CHARGE and PLANT ON PREMISES.

"You want to talk to 702?" Lewis said.

"Yeah, for a minute," Graves said.

Lewis pulled over. Graves got out. The driver in the van wound down his window.

"I hear you're rolling it up," the driver said.

"That's right," Graves said.

"When?"

"Later today."

"What's proto until then?" Proto was slang for protocol.

"Business as usual," Graves said. "Where's 703?"

"Off duty today." The driver shrugged.

"Call them in. I want them to pick up the girl this morning."

"Oh?"

"Yeah."

"Anything else?"

"Yeah. You got some coffee in there?"

"Sure. Two cups?"

Graves looked into the sedan at Lewis. "You want coffee?" Lewis shook his head.

"Just one," Graves said. "Black with four sugars."

The driver sighed and looked into the interior of the dry-cleaning van. "Give the boss his usual," he shouted. A moment later a styrofoam cup was passed out to Graves.

"You're going to catch diabetes," the driver said.

"This is breakfast," Graves said, and walked back to his car. In the background he heard the van driver saying, "702 to 703. Over. 702 to 703. Over."

Graves got in the car, slammed the door. To Lewis: "Let's go."

"The apartment?"

"The apartment."

Wright had taken a fashionable apartment in the hilly north-central section of San Diego, not far from the Cortez Hotel. His building looked out over the city and the harbor. At this hour people were leaving the apartment house, standing in front and waiting until the doorman brought their cars around from the underground garage. Graves had had some trouble getting used to that when he first came here. He was accustomed to the East, where people in cities walked to work or took public transportation. In California, everybody drove. Everybody.

Wright himself was an exception. He had a driver and a limousine. But then, Wright was always an exception, he thought.

Wright usually came out about 8:20. His girl for the night—one of five or six he saw with some frequency—preceded him by ten or fifteen minutes.

"There she is," Lewis said.

Graves nodded. It was odd how you could tell Wright's girls. Even from across the street they could be spotted instantly. Yet there was no particular physical type, no particular details of dress. They weren't professionals. But there was a certain quality about them, something blatantly erotic. They were the girls a man would choose if he wanted to be reassured. Graves watched this one, who wore a simple white dress and had very long legs, as she climbed into a Datsun sportscar and drove off.

"701 to 703," he said, speaking into the intercom mounted on the dash.

There was a crackle of static. "703 here. I thought we could sleep in today."

Graves ignored the complaint. "Red Datsun sportscar, convertible, California license ZVW-348. Got it?"

"Got it. Out."

A moment later, a Ford station wagon drove past them, and the driver gave them the high sign briefly. That was 703.

Graves slumped down in his seat, thinking. They had not bothered to interrogate Wright's girls in recent weeks. When they began, they had had dozens of interviews with the girls. Sometimes they had been straight interrogations; more often they were casually arranged meetings. In both cases the information was monotonously the same. John Wright was a nice and kind and generous and charming man. He was also nervous and definitely conservative. He sweated a lot, preferred the missionary style, kept the room dark, and always remained a little aloof.

Hardly valuable intelligence insight.

"Why do you want this one?" Lewis asked. And then he said, "Here comes the limo."

A black Lincoln limousine pulled up in front of the apartment building. The chauffeur, George Marks, got out, buttoned his uniform jacket, and stood by the door of the passenger side.

Graves had never picked George up for questioning. It had seemed too risky. Now he wondered if that had been a mistake. But he could think of a hundred possible mistakes he had made, especially today. Especially when Wright was being arrested.

"Why are they going to arrest Wright?" Lewis asked. He hadn't gotten an answer on his previous question, so he was trying another.

Graves lit a cigarette. "Phelps is nervous."

"But this computer-tapping business isn't enough—"

"Phelps is running scared just now. There's talk of closing down his division of Intelligence. In fact, the new Secretary is thinking of closing down all State intelligence work."

Lewis raised his eyebrows. "Where'd you hear that?"

Graves smiled. "I'm in Intelligence myself."

Lewis glanced at him a moment, then looked back out the window. A man emerged from the apartment building— stocky, neatly dressed, moving purposefully.

"There's Wright," Lewis said and started the engine of his car.

Graves had watched John Wright get into his limousine every morning for sixty-six days. He knew the routine well: George opened the door and tipped his cap; Wright nodded to him, bent over at the waist, and slipped quickly into the back seat. George closed the door, paused to tug at his leather gloves, and walked around to the driver's side. In the back seat Wright stared straight ahead or opened his newspaper to read.

But this time John Wright stared across the street directly at Graves. And he continued to stare until the limousine moved off in the hot San Diego morning.

Lewis was now very good at following in San Diego traffic; he kept pace three cars back. Graves sat with his arms folded across his chest, frowning. After a time Lewis said, "He was looking at you."

"He certainly was."

"Do you think he's on to us?"

"Impossible," Graves said. He thought of the closet in his apartment. He had five distinctly different suits in that closet, and he rotated them on different days. He thought of the three sedans and the four delivery trucks that the Department used for surveillance work. Different manufacturers, different colors, and a new license plate every week. He had never parked in the same place, never waited for Wright in the same way. He had never presented Wright with a recognizable pattern.

"Impossible," he said again.

And then Graves thought of himself. If he were Wright, would he discover that he was being followed? Even with all the precautions, the safeguards, the changes? He liked to think that he would.

And if he would, why not Wright?

"He's deviating," Lewis said, nodding at the limousine. Graves saw that it was true. Normally on Wednesday mornings Wright went to Balboa Park, where he walked in the gardens, fed the pigeons, and relaxed. But he wasn't doing that today.

He was going downtown.

"Where's our other car?" Graves said.

Lewis picked up the car radio receiver. "701 to 702. Where are you?"

There was a hiss of static. "701, we're at Third and B, going downtown."

Lewis glanced at Graves, who nodded.

"Very good, 702," Lewis said, and clicked off.

The second car, the dry-cleaning van, was running in advance of the limousine. That was standard procedure—one car tailing from the front, one from behind. In cities on really big jobs, they sometimes used four cars, working all around the suspect car. That made it impossible to lose the suspect. But Graves didn't want a four-car tail, and in any case Phelps would never have approved the expense.

The limousine went down Third to Avenue A, then turned left going west.

"702, you have him?"

"We still have him."

Lewis followed the limousine as it went crosstown on A and stopped, pulling up in front of a warehouse. Lewis pulled to the curb half a block behind. They watched as Wright got out and went inside.

Graves lit a cigarette, and they waited. But after only a minute or so, Wright reappeared and got back into his car. The limousine started off.

"Wonder what that was about?" Lewis said.

As they passed the warehouse, Graves read the lettering. He was surprised to find it wasn't a warehouse at all.

BURNS BROS. PLASTICS
VACUUM MOLDING
Containers of all sorts

"Damned if I know," Graves said. He made a note of the name and address in his notebook and then looked up at the street. The limousine was going north now. It went two blocks and turned left, then left again. It pulled up in front of another warehouse.

"It seems he's doing some shopping," Lewis said.

"He's in the wrong part of town."

"I'll drive past," Lewis said, and continued smoothly past the warehouse and the parked limousine. Graves looked out of the corner of his eye. He saw George, the chauffeur, lighting a cigarette. He saw the large glass windows of the warehouse, which was also a salesroom of some kind. Inside he saw Wright standing at the counter receiving a package. In the window were displayed various shining pieces of laboratory equipment.

SANDERSON SCIENTIFIC EQUIPMENT AND SUPPLY
Serving Hospitals and Laboratories
Since 1953

Graves had to smile. Only in California would a date like 1953 seem proof of ageless service to the consumer. "We'll wait for him here," he said, and Lewis pulled over at the end of the block and cut the engine.

Graves checked his watch. It was 8:39. A moment later the limousine sped past them while he was making a note of the scientific supply company and its address. Lewis followed a short distance behind.

The limo again went uptown and pulled over in front of a machine shop. Wright got out and was met at the door by a man carrying a small paper bag. Wright shook hands with the man, who was dressed in dungarees and a blue work shirt. Then Wright opened the paper bag to look inside. He removed one small, shiny metal object, nodded, exchanged a few more words with the man, and got back into his car.

The limousine drove off.

As they passed the machine shop, Graves noted the address and the name. He stared at his list. "A plastics manufacturer, a scientific supply house, and now a machine shop."

"He isn't buying presents for his girls," Lewis said, and laughed.

"Did you check out that purchase last week?" The week

before, Wright had also visited several small industrial manufacturers.

"Yeah," Lewis said. "It was two twelve-foot lengths of
flexible hosing. Very unusual."

"What's unusual about that?"

"It was stainless steel."

"Meaning?"

Lewis shrugged. "The guy I talked to said that nobody
bought flexible stainless steel hosing anymore. People use
either plastic or something like aluminum. Stainless is only
used for piping very corrosive materials."

"Such as?"

"Concentrated dyes, corrosive gases, that kind of thing.
The guy said it was pretty uncommon. Most highly corrosive
stuff is pumped through glass piping. But of course, glass
isn't flexible."

"And Wright bought two lengths of flexible steel?"

"Right. Twelve-foot lengths. At eighty-three dollars a foot."

Graves nodded and watched the car. "He's buying a lot of
specialized equipment. Why?"

"You mean, why is he doing it?"

"No," Graves said. "I mean, why is he doing it himself, in
person?"

"I don't follow you. Why shouldn't he do it himself?"

"Because he's too smart for that," Graves said.

The limousine went uptown twenty blocks and pulled
over in front of another building. The sign said HARRELSON
GARMENTS AND CUSTOM GOODS. They watched Wright get
out of the limo and go inside.

"I'll be goddamned," Graves said.

"What is it?" Lewis said.

"Harrelson was in the papers a year ago. They made

rubber suits and whips and things like that; there was a minor scandal."

Lewis shook his head: "It really is true, then."

"What?"

"About your memory."

Graves shook his head. He'd been through all this before. "I don't have a photographic memory," he said. "I have a better than average memory, that's all."

"Are you trying to convince me?"

"No, just telling you."

"You sound sore."

"You better understand," Graves said, "that I don't have any special powers. None at all. I just plod along, doing a job."

"Here he comes," Lewis said. He pointed to Wright emerging from the store with an armful of packages wrapped in brown paper. George, the chauffeur, jumped out and came around to help carry the packages. Wright indicated that they were to go into the trunk of the car. George locked them there, then came around, shut Wright's door, and drove off.

"I'd like to know what was in those packages," Graves said, making notes in his book.

"Bet you anything it's kinky rubber clothing," Lewis said.

"What will you bet?"

At that, Lewis laughed. He knew you didn't bet with Graves. Nobody bet with Graves. He might deny special skills until he was blue in the face, but the fact was that Graves was the best gambler, bettor, poker player that any of them had ever seen.

They followed the car for another five minutes. Then it pulled up in front of a sporting goods store. Wright again got out. He said something to George, who nodded and went across the street to a coffee shop. The car was left alone. It could not be seen easily from either the sports store or the coffee shop.

"Looks like we have our chance," Graves said. "Pull over."

As Lewis pulled the sedan over, Graves opened the glove compartment and took out a large, circular key ring. On it were keys to Wright's apartment in New York, his apartment in San Diego, his limousine, his Alfa sportscar, his summer house in Southampton, his winter house in Jamaica. And several others as well. They were all neatly tagged.

Lewis said, "Isn't this a little risky—"

"We're going to arrest him today," Graves said. "It doesn't matter now." He got out of the car, feeling the heat of the morning air. He walked forward to the limousine. It took just a moment to insert his key in the trunk and open it. He raised the trunk lid partway and looked at the brown paper packages. There were three, closed with strips of tape. He opened a corner of one and peered inside.

The package contained black rubber belts, about 6 inches wide, formed into loops of varying diameters. He closed the package and squeezed the others. They all seemed to contain belts.

Frowning, he shut the trunk. And then, because he was in a gambling mood, he walked into the sporting goods store. As he went through the door he glanced back at Lewis. Lewis looked horrified.

The store was large and spacious; he did not see Wright immediately. Walking among the aisles of equipment, he finally spotted him in the water sports department. Wright was gesturing with his hands, forming a shape in the air.

Graves walked over and stood beside him at the counter. To do so gave Graves an immediate burst of excitement. He had never been so close to his subject before. Wright was smaller than he had thought—several inches shorter than Graves himself. And much finer-boned. A delicate man in an English-cut suit, dapper as Phelps, but without the vanity that made Phelps unbearable.

The salesman said, "I'll be right with you, sir," and Graves nodded.

Wright glanced over at him and smiled vaguely. There was no recognition in the glance. None at all: Graves was sure of it. They were just two customers at the same counter.

Graves bent over, peering down at the glass case, which contained depth gauges and underwater watches. He could see Wright's face reflected in the glass surface.

"Is this the one you mean, sir?" the salesman asked.

Graves glanced up and saw the salesman holding a small air tank, painted yellow.

"That's the one," Wright said.

"Now, do you understand about this tank?" the salesman said. "It's not the standard seventy-two cubic foot model. This one only has twenty-five minutes of air at—"

"That's the one I want." Wright said it quietly, but his voice cut the salesman off. Graves was impressed by the understated authority in the voice—and presumably in the man.

"Yes, sir. How many was that?"

"Three."

"I think we have three in the storeroom," the salesman said. He turned to Graves: "Was there anything in particular?"

It seemed to Graves that the salesman was much less deferential to him than he was to Wright. But perhaps he was being paranoid.

"I need a depth gauge," Graves said.

"They're all down there," the salesman said, pointing to

the case. "Be with you in a minute. Three, was it, sir? I'll get them."

The salesman walked off.

After a moment Graves said, "I don't know anything about this."

There was a short, ambiguous pause. Finally Wright said, "Diving?"

"Yes. It's a present for my son."

"He does a lot of diving?" Wright was being formal, polite, barely interested.

Wait until I put the handcuffs on, Graves thought. "Oh, he's a nut about it, but he doesn't really get much chance. Twice a year during school vacations we go down to Mexico. That's really all."

Wright said, "That one there is a good one." He pointed to a gauge in the case.

Graves nodded. "I really don't know anything about this," he repeated.

"You don't dive yourself?"

"No," Graves said. "It always seemed too dangerous to me."

"There's a certain thrill in danger, though."

"Not for me. Not at my age."

"You prefer golf?"

"Poker," Graves said, and looked directly at Wright for the first time.

Wright smiled. "Poker can be very challenging," he said. "But it's like any other game. If you get too good, you're limited in your opponents."

"Yes, I've found that."

"You're good?" There was just the slightest taunt in the voice, the slightest goading.

"Yes, I'm good," Graves found himself saying.

For a moment the two men exchanged a level, appraising look. Wright broke it; he looked down at the counter. "Still," he said, "I admire the young, with their exuberance in physical sports. It raises the stakes. You can be hurt, you can be injured. You can even be killed."

"But when you're young, you don't think of that. It doesn't matter."

"Oh," Wright said, "I think it always matters. Dying always matters."

The salesman came back. "You're in luck, Mr. Johnson," he said cheerfully. "You got the last three tanks. Shall I have them put in your car?"

"That will be fine," Wright said, smiling.

"You must be out of your mind," Lewis said. They were back in the car, following the limousine.

"Not at all."

"I suppose you went up and talked to him."

"As a matter of fact, I did."

Lewis smiled. "I know you've been doing this a long time, but still…"

"Look," Graves said, "we're picking him up later today."

"But you're teasing him, playing a game…"

"Of course," Graves said.

The limousine went up Avenue D and pulled to a stop in front of a large hotel. A man came out, bent over the limo, and talked to Wright in the back seat. The conversation lasted several minutes. Finally the man turned and went inside. The limousine pulled away from the curb.

Graves snatched up the microphone. "701 to 702."

"702 here."

"He's all yours from now on. Stick to him. Out."

Lewis looked stunned. "What the—"

Graves pointed to the figure of the man going back into the hotel. "Follow that man and see where he goes. His name is Timothy Drew."

San Diego: 9 a.m. PDT
Hour 8

"Hold out your hands."

Peters held out his hands and waited while the supervisor ran the Geiger counter over them. It made a soft clicking sound in the cavernous warehouse garage.

"Stand still."

He stood and watched as the counter probe was passed over his chest, his abdomen, his legs. It was a little like being frisked.

"Turn around."

He turned. He heard the counter clicking as it was passed down his spine to his feet.

"Okay. Next."

Peters stepped aside, and the driver moved forward. As the driver was being checked by the Geiger counter, the dispatcher said to Peters, "First run?"

"Yes," Peters said.

"Ever done a DC before?"

Peters pointed to the counter. "Not like this."

"What've you done, explosives?"

"Yes."

"This is easier than explosives or flammables," the dispatcher said. "We've got a regulation for two men in the cab, and another for staying under forty-five miles an hour. That's it. We can take all the roads, all the tunnels and bridges. Much easier than explosives."

Peters nodded. "What exactly is it?"

The dispatcher consulted his clipboard. "Mostly hospital

supplies. Cases of intravenous saline, twelve quarts to the case, thirty cases in all. Cases of penicillin G, forty-eight ampoules to the case, fifteen cases in all. And two rad cartridges."

"Rad cartridges?"

"Two bars of plutonium-238 oxide. That's a radioactive isotope. One thousand grams each—they're packed in lead cylinders."

"That's our dangerous cargo?" Peters asked.

"You bet," the dispatcher said.

The driver finished his check and came over to join them. "What was that all about?"

"Insurance," the dispatcher said. "You have to be cleared before exposure to the cargo, in order for our coverage to be effective. We should also do a blood test, but we don't bother." He turned to Peters. "Reeves, this is your rider, Peters. Peters, Reeves."

Reeves shook hands with Peters. As he did so he gave him a slightly surprised look, as if something were mildly wrong.

The dispatcher nodded across the warehouse. "Truck's over there," he said. "Have a good trip."

Peters blinked in the sun and put on his sunglasses. Beside him, Reeves sighed. "Bright day," he said.

"Sure is."

"You new at this?"

"Yeah."

"What'd you do before?"

"Airplane tail assembly. Lockheed, in Palmdale."

"Tail assembly, huh?" Reeves said, and laughed loudly.

"They laid me off."

Reeves stopped laughing and nodded sympathetically.

"Rough," he said. And then after a moment, "Laid off the tail assembly." And he chuckled some more.

Peters smiled. He felt confident about Reeves, who was fat and sloppy and casual—and fifteen years his senior. There wouldn't be any difficulty.

"Well," Reeves said, "since you're new at this, you might as well learn the ropes." He reached into his pocket and withdrew a plastic bottle of yellow pills. He handed it to Peters.

"What's this?" Peters asked.

"Dex. Go ahead, take one. Feel terrific."

Peters shook a pill into his hand and paused. Reeves took one, then reached into his leather jacket and produced a flask.

"Wash it down with this," he said. "Vodka. No smell." He handed Peters the flask.

Peters dropped the pill from his hand, letting it roll down between the seats. He pretended to swig from the flask, then returned it to Reeves.

"You'll learn," the driver said, and smiled.

Peters nodded and leaned forward slightly in his seat. That way he could see out the side-view mirror and keep an eye on the black Ford sedan that had been following them for the past fifteen minutes.

Ten minutes later they were on the San Diego Freeway, moving down the far right lane. They passed a green-and-silver sign: HACKLEY RD. EXIT 1 MILE. Peters shifted in his seat. Reeves was talking about his children.

"They're good kids," he was saying, "but they don't show proper respect. All this screaming about the President, all this revolution talk, it makes me want to—"

"We get off at the next exit," Peters said.

"No," Reeves said, "we don't stop for another—" He broke off.

Peters had taken the pistol from the pocket of his leather jacket.

"Hackley Road," Peters said quietly. "Turn off the ramp and go half a mile east. You'll see a small dirt road. Turn right onto that."

"I'll be goddamned," the driver said.

They came to Hackley Road and turned off on the exit ramp. They drove east. Peters glanced in the side mirror and saw that the Ford sedan was still following.

"I should have known," Reeves said.

"How's that?"

"I should have known something was wrong when I shook hands. It's your hands."

"What about them?"

"They're soft as a baby's ass," Reeves said. "You never worked in your life."

"Turn right, up here," Peters said.

It went smoothly. Reeves pulled the truck onto the dirt road and stopped in a clump of eucalyptus trees. Peters made Reeves get out and lie on his stomach on the ground, with his hands over his head.

Reeves said nothing for a long time. Finally he said, "You going to shoot me?"

"Not if you stay quiet," Peters said.

The Ford sedan drew up behind the truck and three men, all wearing children's Halloween masks, jumped out. A driver remained at the wheel. Nobody spoke as the men opened the back of the truck, climbed up on the hydraulic tailgate, and went into the cargo area.

"Nice and easy," Peters said, standing near Reeves with the gun. "Nice and easy."

Reeves did not move.

The men emerged from the truck carrying two small, extremely heavy boxes. Peters could see the triple-blade radiation symbol on the boxes. The men closed the truck and started to load the boxes into the car. One of them came over and expertly tied and gagged Reeves with adhesive tape.

Then, speaking for the first time, the man said, "Let's go."

Peters was confused. "I thought you were going to take—"

"Let's go."

Peters went with the man, who wore a Donald Duck mask, and got into the car. The sedan backed out of the road and drove off.

The men all left their masks on. One of them said, "What's the time?"

"Nine thirty-two."

"Perfect."

Peters was given a mask of his own, a witch's mask with day-glo pink cheeks and wild eyes. He pulled it on and said, "I thought we were taking the penicillin too."

"The plan was changed," somebody said.

"But if we just take the capsules—"

"The plan was changed this morning. We were told to take only the capsules."

Peters frowned and said nothing. He felt the change in plan was a terrible mistake. By stealing the penicillin they would have confused the issue; it might have taken the truckers several days to discover the theft of the radiation capsules. But now they'd find only the capsules gone...It was too obvious, too simple. Why had the change been made?

"Time?"

"Nine thirty-six."

The driver nodded and pulled over to the side of the road. The men sat quietly, not removing their masks. Peters looked at the backs of their necks, noticing the length of their hair, the condition of their collars, the way they were dressed. Several minutes passed.

"Time?"

"Nine forty."

The driver put the car in gear. He drove down the road through gently rolling farm country. The morning air was still cool.

"There it is."

Up ahead was another dirt road turnoff, with another truck pulled off the road and another man standing over the driver.

"Remember, we want twenty pounds of it."

The black sedan pulled up behind the truck. Peters was given the spool of inch-wide adhesive tape; he quickly tied and gagged the driver. Meanwhile the others opened the truck and removed several small packages. They were wrapped in clear plastic and looked like bread dough: a whitish, putty-like substance. The men carried two packages each, bringing them around to the trunk of the sedan, setting them in carefully, then going back for more.

Peters gave a mask to the man standing over the driver with the gun. The gunman did not speak. Then Peters went around to the trunk of the sedan and began counting the plastic packages. When there were twenty, he placed them in a suitcase, locked the case, and closed the trunk.

The men climbed back into the sedan and drove off,

"Time?"

"Nine fifty-one."

"Beautiful."

The black sedan drove back to the San Diego Freeway and stopped at the on-ramp for Hackley Road. Peters got out. So did the other gunman. Peters went around to the trunk and removed the suitcase with the plastic packages. The other gunman placed the two radiation capsules into the blue canvas gym bag.

He stood with Peters until the sedan had pulled onto the freeway and disappeared. Then, his back to the road, he took off his mask. Peters took off his mask as well. The other man removed a paper American flag from the bag. With Peters's help, he taped the flag onto the side of the suitcase.

Then Peters removed his black-haired wig and his moustache. The other man removed his blond wig and peeled away a reddish, new-looking scar on the side of his cheek.

The two men looked at each other and laughed.

"Well done, brother," Peters said, and clapped him on the back.

They waited five minutes, and then another black sedan, very dusty, pulled up. An older man leaned out and said, "Give you boys a lift?"

Peters said, "We're going to Phoenix." As he said it, he glanced at his brother, who was frowning.

"Hell of a long way," the old man said. "Anyhow, you want to go south. This is the north ramp."

"We're just resting a minute."

The man looked at them as if they were peculiar, shrugged, and drove onto the ramp. His car rattled as he gathered speed, and then he was gone. They were left by the roadside.

His brother lit a cigarette.

"You know," his brother said, "this is going to create a hell of a mess."

"That was the idea."

"When are you leaving?"

"Four."

"That's cutting it awfully close. I'm getting out at three."

"To Vegas?"

His brother nodded. "You?"

"Chicago."

"You better hope nothing delays that plane on the ground."

"There's another flight at four thirty. I'm booked on that one as well."

His brother nodded.

Down the road they saw a car approach. It was black and white, a sedan. They couldn't see it clearly, but as it came closer they saw the configuration better. A police car.

"Shit," Peters said.

His brother lit another cigarette. "What if he wants to look in the suitcase? What if he—"

"We haven't done anything wrong," Peters said. He glanced at his watch. It was almost ten o'clock. Where the hell was the pickup?

The police car came closer.

"I don't like this at all," his brother said.

"We haven't done anything wrong," Peters said again.

The police car approached them and put on its blinker.

"The bastard's pulling over."

But the car did not pull over. Instead, it drove onto the ramp and merged with traffic. The cop hardly glanced at them.

They sighed.

"What time is it?"

"I have ten, on the nose."

In the distance a car got off the far ramp and made a U-turn under the freeway. It was a Cadillac convertible with a woman driving. She came around and started up the ramp, going back the way she had come. She stopped when she saw them.

"I took the wrong turnoff. Can I give you fellows a lift?"

"We're going to Phoenix," Peters said.

"No kidding," the woman said. "That's my home town."

"No kidding," Peters said, "Which part?"

"The right part," she said.

The two men exchanged glances, then got into the car, placing the suitcases in the back seat. The woman said, "Sorry I'm late," and drove off. Nothing else was said.

San Diego: 10 a.m. PDT

Hour 7

The voice crackled over the telephone line. "Fucking around with the computers," Phelps said, "is not my idea of a joke."

Graves sat in the hotel phone booth and stared across the lobby at Lewis and a marshal. Lewis was gesturing to Graves to get off the phone. "It wasn't intended as a joke."

"How was it intended?" Phelps said, his voice heavy with sarcasm.

"It was intended as an attempt to recall my own file."

"You're not supposed to do that."

"There are a lot of things I'm not supposed to do."

"And you seem bent on doing all of them," Phelps said. "Have you picked up Wright yet?"

"No."

"You've certainly had time; it's ten—"

"I want to play him a little. Besides, I have somebody else."

"Oh?"

"Timothy Drew."

"Where?"

"Upstairs. We've got him in a hotel room on Third."

"We've been looking for him for forty-eight hours," Phelps said. "And I mean looking *hard*. How did you find him?"

"Wright led us to him," Graves said. That was the only thing that bothered Graves. It was too much like a setup, as if Wright were giving him Drew.

"How convenient," Phelps said. "When are you going to arrest him?"

"He's already arrested. The federal marshals are up there with him."

"I mean Wright."

"Later in the day," Graves said.

"You and your goddamned poker games," Phelps said. "I want you to call me in an hour."

"All right."

"Stop agreeing with me. Just do it." And he hung up.

Graves left the phone booth. Lewis came over with his notebook open. They headed for the elevator.

"What've you got?" Graves said.

"It's pretty strange," Lewis said. "At Sanderson's today, Wright bought a Model 477 scintillation counter. Retail price, two hundred forty-seven dollars."

"A scintillation counter?"

"Yeah. It's apparently a kind of high-grade Geiger counter. Reads radiation."

"Does it have any other uses?"

"Nobody knows of any."

"What else?"

"The machine shop ground three fittings for him to custom specifications. All high-grade stainless steel. Two of them are on-off pressure valves with special handles. The third is a T coupling which brings together two hoses into a common outlet."

"What's special about the valve handles?"

"The handles have a series of perforations, presumably so the valves can be turned on and off by some sort of machine."

"Any information about what kind of machine would be used to turn the valves on and off?"

Lewis shook his head. "But they said the handles are spring-loaded. A moderate pressure will snap them from full shut to the full open position."

"Now that's really interesting," Graves said. "You mean there are no intermediate positions for the valves?"

"Yes. It's either full shut or full open."

The elevator came. Graves pressed the button for the sixth floor.

"When did Wright order these custom fittings?"

"Last week. Rush order."

"Really interesting," Graves said. "What about the plastics store?"

Lewis scratched his head. "Three weeks ago Wright ordered two pressure-molded plastic tanks from them. Long tanks roughly a foot in diameter and eight feet long. Specified as triple-laminate things able to withstand pressures up to five hundred pounds per square inch. The shop was surprised to get the order."

"Why?"

"Well, the guy said nobody orders tanks like that in plastic. It's too dangerous. All high-pressure tanks are metal and seamless. There's no advantage to plastic, even in weight. Plastic tanks, if they're triple-thickness, are heavier than metal."

"Wright wouldn't order something that had no advantage."

"Well," Lewis said, "the guy thought Wright was a pretty strange customer. Not only did he want these plastic tanks, but he wanted them made out of allacron."

"Which is?"

"A very tough, resilient plastic, but highly combustible. It burns like a bastard, so it isn't used much."

"Have the tanks been finished?"

"They were delivered a week ago to a private airfield hangar in El Cajon, about twelve miles from here."

"You have the address?"

"Yeah. I tried to call; no telephone there."

Graves frowned. He was more convinced than ever that Wright was playing with him, leading him on a chase, daring him to put the puzzle together.

Two high-pressure tanks of combustible plastic.

Special steel fittings, including a T nozzle.

Two steel hoses, flexible.

All that made a kind of sense. You had two tanks, and two hoses that joined in a T nozzle, so that the contents of the two tanks—liquid or gas, presumably—would come together at the T nozzle and then be expelled as a mixture.

That was easy to visualize.

But what was the point? And what was the point of the skin-diving tanks, and the rubber strips, and the Geiger counter?

The elevator stopped at the sixth floor. They both got out and walked to Drew's room.

"Where is Wright now?"

"I just checked with 702. He's in that apartment on Alameda."

"The one he rented last week?"

"Right."

The newly rented apartment was also a puzzle. Wright had apparently leased it on the spur of the moment. It seemed to coincide with nothing, except with the fact that one girl had been seen leaving his old apartment near the Cortez Hotel three mornings in a row. This was unusual enough to suggest that Wright was going to set her up as his mistress.

"702 talked to the doorman. Wright told the doorman they'd be moving furniture into the apartment later in the day."

"Hmmm." That seemed totally unreasonable to Graves. Wright wouldn't spend time supervising domestic arrangements for a girl. It was beneath him.

Stopping in the hallway, Lewis said, "Does all this make sense to you?"

"No," Graves said. "Not yet. But I expect to get some help."

Without knocking he opened the door and entered Drew's room.

❖

Timothy Drew sat in an overstuffed chair and said, "I want to see my lawyer." His voice was calm. The fact of his arrest, and the presence of two federal marshals standing by the doors with their hands resting on the butts of their revolvers, did not seem to disturb him at all.

Graves's eyes swept the living room. It was an expensive hotel suite, furnished in a heavily elegant style. Altogether, not bad for a man one year out of the Army. He sat down in a chair opposite Drew.

"I want to see my lawyer," Drew repeated. His eyes flicked once to Graves, then went back to the cops, as if he had decided Graves was unimportant.

"You'll have that opportunity," Graves said.

Drew's eyes snapped back, fixed on him.

"In due time," Graves added.

"I want to do it now."

"We're in a hurry," Graves said. His voice was not hurried at all. "We'd prefer to have a statement from you now."

"I have nothing to say."

Graves shrugged, and lit a cigarette. He never took his eyes off Drew. This was going to be a kind of chess game, he knew, and it was a game he could win if he kept his temper.

"I want to see my lawyer," Drew repeated.

Graves did not reply. He just stared. That was the simplest form of pressure, and he wanted to see if it would work.

"Listen," Drew said, "who are you guys, anyway? You haven't got the right to push me around. You haven't got a warrant—"

"Did you show him the warrant?" Graves said.

"Yeah, we showed him the warrant," one of the marshals said.

"Show him again."

The marshal snapped open the warrant in front of Drew, then took it away.

"Signed by a federal district court judge at nine thirty this morning," Graves said. "All in order, all perfectly legal. You're arrested on a charge of conspiracy to steal classified information. It carries a mandatory twenty-year prison sentence if you're convicted. Parole is not granted for such charges. Do you know what that means?"

"I want to see my lawyer."

"I'm trying to help you," Graves said quietly. "Keep your mouth shut and listen: You were observed tampering with the computer terminals at Southern California Underwriters. You tapped into classified data banks at known times which coincide with your access to the terminals in question. We have traced back the lines. Furthermore, you utilized certain codes known to you but outdated. This gives you away. It's quite straightforward. You'll get out of prison when you're about fifty."

Graves stood up. "Now think carefully, Mr. Drew. Is it worth it?"

Drew's face went blank, neutral, composed. "I want to see my lawyer."

Graves sighed and walked around the living room, looking idly at details. He glanced into the bedroom and saw a packed suitcase next to the bed. He looked back at Drew. "Planning a trip?"

"I want to see my lawyer."

Graves walked into the bedroom and opened the suitcase. The bottom half was filled with lightweight clothing, bathing trunks, sports clothes.

The top was packed with money, neat stacks of twenty-dollar bills held tight in paper sleeves. Fresh from the bank. He counted the stacks: it came to roughly twenty thousand dollars.

In a corner of the bedroom draped over a chair was a sports coat. He found a ticket for the noon plane to Acapulco in the pocket. A first-class ticket, one-way.

He returned to the living room. Drew watched him, wary now.

"Planning a trip, Mr. Drew?"

"I want to see my lawyer."

"That's a lot of money in there, Mr. Drew."

"I have nothing to say."

"From your ticket, it looks like you were planning to stay down there. Not come back."

Drew shook his head. He did not speak. He was sweating, but still in control; he showed no sign of cracking.

"Can you account for all that money?"

"No comment. I want to see—"

"All right," Graves said. He sighed and turned to the marshals. "Okay, lock him up."

The marshals grabbed Drew roughly, each taking an arm. For the first time Drew became excited: "What's going on?"

Graves found the reaction interesting. Was Drew afraid of jail? Was he homosexual? Did he need drugs? Graves decided to play on the jail fear. "We don't have many options, Mr. Drew. I know it's not pleasant, but we've got to put you in jail. You know, there's a lot of paperwork, and sometimes people get lost. Inadvertently deprived of their rights. I mean, people have spent a day or two in jail, and their papers get mixed up. So they don't get any food, or water, or anything. But you see, nobody knows you're there. For a while."

"Where are you taking me?" Drew's voice was strained now, very tense.

"Downtown. We'll be talking to you again in a day or so, when you're more...relaxed."

"*Downtown San Diego?*"

"Yes," Graves said. And he suddenly realized that Drew wasn't afraid of jail at all. He didn't want to stay in the city. That was what he was afraid of.

"You can't do that!"

"Just watch it happen," Graves said, lighting a cigarette.

"I've got to leave," Drew said. He was now openly agitated. "I have to leave. I have to leave."

"Why?"

"It's my sister. She's sick, in Mexico. That's why I have the money, I need it—"

"You don't have a sister," Graves said. "You have one brother two years older than you, who sells insurance in Portland, Oregon. Your father is still alive and lives in Michigan. Your mother died two years ago of a heart attack."

Drew's body sagged.

"Put him down," Graves said to the marshals. They dropped him back into the chair. "Now listen to me," Graves said. "You aren't going anywhere without giving us some help."

Drew stared at him. "I want a cigarette."

Graves gave him one.

"What time is it now?" Drew asked dully.

"Ten thirty." Graves lit the cigarette for him and watched as Drew sat back and inhaled.

"Listen," Drew said, "I have to catch that plane at noon."

"Why is that?" Graves said.

"I don't know," Drew said. "I swear to God I don't know."

"What do you know?"

"I know I have to get out of San Diego today, because… something is going to happen."

"How do you know this?"

"John told me."

"John Wright?"

"Yes."

"What did he say?"

"He said that the binary would go off today. In San Diego."

"And what is the binary?"

"I don't know." He sucked on the cigarette.

"Mr. Drew, you're going to have to do better—"

"I swear to you, I don't know."

Graves paused. He let Drew sweat, and let him smoke. Finally he said, "How is the binary related to the information you tapped from the data banks?"

"I can't be sure. The information was in two areas. One was easy to get, the other was hard. First, John wanted supply routings. I spent a couple of days learning how to plug into the subroutines to release the information. I kept getting 'no authorization' printouts, but finally I managed to plug in."

"And extract what?"

"Supply routings for different things."

"Things?"

"Well, John gave me the codes for what he wanted. Don't ask me where he got those codes. One of the codes was for a thing called 'Binary 75 slash 76.' I got a supply routing for that."

"And you have no idea what the code represents?"

"None. Except that it's obviously Defense Department material, transported by rail."

"How do you know that?"

"From the routings themselves. You can't be sure what's being transported, but you can tell the method—air, rail, other surface vehicle, truck convoy. You can tell the method."

"What else can you tell?"

"You can tell the C and C ratings."

"What's that?"

"Command and Control provides a rating for all material transportation. The ratings are in grades: grades one through seven. One is pretty safe, or pretty inexpensive. Like clothing, or spare auto parts—that sort of thing. Seven is very expensive or very dangerous."

"What was Binary 75 slash 76?"

"It was a grade seven."

"What did you think Binary 75 slash 76 represented?"

Drew puffed on his cigarette. He did not answer for a long time. Finally he said, "I thought it was radioactive materials."

"Meaning?"

"I don't know. Components for a bomb, maybe. I don't know."

Graves almost immediately rejected that explanation, although it fitted with the scintillation counter.

"What else could it be?"

"You asked me what I thought it was. I told you."

"You think Wright planned to make an atomic bomb?"

"I think he planned to steal the components. Maybe he already has."

"And do what with them?"

"I don't know. But it's going to happen today."

Graves sat back. Drew put out his cigarette. Graves offered him another.

"What does a code like 'binary' mean?"

"It could be just a random code," Drew said. "But they usually have some specific meaning. That's why I thought it was atomic components."

"Binary…"

"Meaning a twin system," Drew said. "Something with

two active parts, two units. Nuclear bombs are like that. You have two sections of uranium, neither of which will explode by itself. But you bring them together, and you reach critical mass, start a chain reaction." He snapped his fingers. "Bingo."

By now Graves was convinced that Drew believed this explanation. Graves did not. Whatever Wright planned, it had nothing to do with atomic bombs. That didn't fit with the tanks and hoses and nozzles, all of which pointed to some gas or liquid apparatus.

"He's insane," Drew said suddenly. "That's the trouble. He's crazy. He's convinced that everybody is out to get him, and he's convinced that the government is being turned over to the wrong elements, and he's convinced that only he can set things right."

"You mentioned that there was something else you had to tap from the data banks. What was it?"

"That was strange," Drew said. "I'd already tapped the Defense routings. My job was over. Then John asked me to tap into the State data banks."

"State?"

"State Department. I said I couldn't. He told me to try, and gave me some more codes. I don't know where he got those either, but they worked."

"What was the information he wanted?"

"File summary on one person," Drew said. "A man who worked in State Department Intelligence named Graves."

"I see," Graves said. "Did you obtain the information?"

"Eventually."

"And you gave it to Wright?"

"Yes. He wasn't interested in it, I don't think, except for one part. The psychological test scores."

"Do you remember anything else?"

"No. Only that John was very interested in the psychological tests." He puffed on the cigarette. "I remember he said when he saw it, 'Well, this is the final cog in the machine,' and laughed."

"What did he mean by that?"

"Damned if I know," Drew said.

San Diego: 11 *a.m. PDT*

Hour 6

As they left Drew's room, Lewis said, "By the way, they're still holding the girl."

"The girl?" Graves was distracted, thinking about what Drew had said.

"The girl we picked up this morning."

"Oh yes. Where is she?"

"They've got her downstairs. In the grand ballroom."

Graves nodded and checked his watch. They'd held the girl for several hours already. "I'd better see her now," he said. "What's her name?"

Lewis consulted his notes. "Cynthia Lembeck."

"How does she seem?"

Lewis shrugged. "Nervous."

Anyone would be nervous, Graves thought, who had to spend much time in the hotel's grand ballroom. It was a cavernous space with ornate walls and ceiling, but for some reason all the tables and chairs had been removed. The ballroom was empty except for a girl sitting in a fold-up chair near one wall, and a marshal standing nearby.

Graves went over to her.

Seen close, she was darkly tanned, conventionally pretty, and older than he had expected—in her late twenties or early thirties.

"Miss Lembeck?"

"Oh," she said in surprise. "It's you."

That stopped him. Stopped him cold. "You recognize me?"

"Well, just your face. I've seen your picture."

"Where?"

"John's apartment."

"I see."

"Are you a friend of his?"

"Not exactly," Graves said. "I work for the government."

"Something to do with the Convention?"

"Not exactly." He switched into a straightforward interrogation mode. "How long have you known Mr. Wright, Miss Lembeck?"

"About a month."

"How did you meet him?"

"Through friends." She glanced from Graves to the marshal. "Have I done something wrong?"

"No, no. We just want to ask you some questions. What can you tell us about Mr. Wright?"

"He's very nice," she said. "We're engaged."

"Oh?" That was a surprise.

"Yes. He bought me an apartment, just last week."

"I see."

"It's very nice. At least, it will be."

The girl was not very bright, but she had a sweet sexiness that was unmistakable. Still, he couldn't imagine Wright marrying her. In the past he had married well-known women, celebrities.

"There's nothing there now," the girl said. "They're moving furniture in today."

"You must be excited."

"Oh, I am. John's excited, too. But he has so much on his mind."

"How do you mean?"

"Well, business things. He's very interested in politics, you know."

"No, I didn't know that."

"You didn't?" She seemed puzzled. "I thought—well, anyway, he is. And this morning, we had the news on the television, and they announced that the President was coming into town. Well, he got very upset, and started making telephone calls. A lot of them."

"What sort of calls?"

"I don't know. They were long distance."

"Did you hear any of them?"

"No."

"Are you sure?"

"Well, I heard him ask the operator for area code 801. That's Washington, isn't it?"

"Yes," Graves said. He knew that it wasn't, but he could check it later.

"He was very upset. And then later, he mentioned China. He doesn't like the President about China, you know." She sighed. "He thinks it's very wrong."

"I see. You say you've seen my picture—"

"Only last night," she said. "That was the first time. I thought you were related to him or something. Because he has your picture up all over the place."

"This happened last night?"

"Yes. But he was strange last night, anyway. Nervous."

"I see. What about?"

"I don't know. He's worried about business things. He said something about a shipment he's expecting."

"What else was strange, last night?"

She hesitated, apparently embarrassed.

"Go on," Graves said gently.

"Well, it was different last night. He was very…vigorous. He did it three times."

"I see," Graves said.

*

Outside the ballroom Lewis was in a phone booth, checking the area code. He came out and fell into step with Graves. "Eight oh one," he said, "is Utah."

"Any particular place?"

"No. The whole state is one area code."

"Shit," Graves said. "I wish we had a tap on his phone."

"Well, we did our best to get it," Lewis reminded him.

"Yeah," Graves said. He sighed. "I never thought I'd hear myself complaining because we hadn't tapped a phone."

"Things are different now," Lewis said.

"They sure are."

They went outside into the bright hot morning sun and climbed into the car. Lewis started the engine. "Where to?"

"Miss Lembeck's new apartment. The one Wright just rented."

"Okay," Lewis said.

When they arrived at the apartment building, they saw Wright's limousine parked in front. Behind the wheel George was reading a newspaper.

"Are we fully set up across the street?" Graves said.

"We should be," Lewis said.

Graves nodded. "Wait here. I'll go see what they've found."

The day before, they had set up a surveillance unit in the apartment building facing Wright's. Graves rode to the nineteenth floor, got out, and walked to Room 1905. He knocked once.

"Who is it?"

"Graves."

The door was opened for him. He entered the room. It was small and bare except for equipment clustered around the windows. There were two sets of binoculars on tripods and three sets of cameras; four chairs; a directional microphone, also on a tripod; recording equipment; film canisters; heaping ashtrays. And a television set.

On the TV Walter Cronkite was saying, "—are trying to get a vote from the Alabama delegation, which is apparently still in caucus." In the background a booming, echoing mechanical voice was saying, "Alabama…Alabama…Alabama…"

Graves ignored the TV. "What've you got?" he asked.

One of the three men in the room stepped away from the binoculars. "Have a look," he said.

Graves looked.

From this vantage point he could see directly into one window of Wright's apartment on the nineteenth floor of the opposite building. There were no drapes on the window, which made it easy to see in. The room was bare except for four peculiar wooden structures standing in the center of the floor.

"They had drapes on that window too," the man said, "but they took them off half an hour ago."

"From all the windows?"

"No. Just this one."

Graves frowned. Why? Did they know they were being observed? Did they want to make it easier? Because that was what they had done. He could see Wright striding around the room, directing two other people. Wright was working in shirtsleeves.

"The window's open," Graves said. "It must be hot as hell in there."

"That's right," the man said. "The window has been open ever since Wright showed up. An hour ago."

"What're those wooden things on the floor?"

"Sawhorses," the man said. "We figure they had paperhangers in there. Paperhangers use sawhorses. But there's something funny going on."

"How do you mean?"

"Well, look at the sawhorses closely. They have indentations cut in them."

Graves looked. He could see a broadly curved, U-shaped cut in each sawhorse.

"Why?"

"Beats me. They just cut them a while back."

"You mean, specially?"

"That's right. They've been doing a lot of unusual things in there. Every so often Wright sticks his hand out the window, and he's got this whirling thing, like a kid's whirling top... He sticks his hand out there for a minute, then pulls it back."

Graves looked away from the window. "Describe it exactly."

"It has four arms," the man said, "and at the end of each is a cup, to catch the wind. Sort of a weathervane. But there isn't much wind today."

"Anemometer," Graves said.

"A what?"

"It measures wind velocity." Why should Wright want to know the wind velocity outside the window of his girlfriend's apartment?

"Why does he care about that?" the man said.

Graves shook his head and turned back to the window, examining the sawhorses through the binoculars. Each sawhorse with its single indentation in the crossbar.

Four sawhorses.

Two tanks. Of course! The crossbars would have indentations so that the tank wouldn't roll off. "You seen any tanks in there?"

"Nothing like that," the man said. "All we've seen is a lot of mechanical equipment."

"What kind of mechanical equipment?" Graves peered through the binoculars. He didn't see any equipment at all.

"It looks like pumps and stuff," the man said. "It was right in the middle of the floor." He glanced through the binoculars, then shook his head. "They must have moved it to another room. They had some electronic equipment, too."

"What kind?"

"Looked like a hi-fi, maybe."

Graves thought of several nasty remarks, but said nothing. A hi-fi, for Christ's sake.

"That guy in there must be pretty weird," the man said.

Graves turned on him. "He is not weird. He is a brilliant and a dedicated man. He is engaged in a complicated plot and he is daring—" He broke off. The man was staring. "He's not weird," Graves finished, and returned to the binoculars.

As he watched, John Wright stepped to the window and extended his hand. He held an anemometer; the cups spun lazily. After a moment Wright withdrew the instrument and returned to directing the other men in the room.

Graves turned away from the window and made some calls.

"Department of Defense."

"Public Information, please."

"Just a minute, please." There was a clicking.

"Public Information, Miss Conover speaking."

"I'd like to talk to Lieutenant Morrison, please."

"One minute, please." More clicking.

"Lieutenant Morrison's office."

"John Graves calling for Lieutenant Morrison."

"Just a minute, I'll see if he's in." Still more clicking.

"Morrison here. What is it?" As usual, Morrison sounded harried.

"Pete, this is John Graves at State. I'm in San Diego, and I need some information."

"Shoot."

"Pete, I need to know what a code word represents. The code word is Binary 75 slash 76."

Morrison coughed in surprise. "Where'd you hear that?"

"Pete, just tell me what it means."

"Jesus, this is an open line."

"I know it's an open line. Tell me what it means."

"Where are you calling from?"

"San Diego."

"Jesus, you must be out of your mind."

"I need the information, Pete. And I need it now."

"Look," Morrison said, "if you don't mind me saying so, this is pretty irregular. You've just popped a—" He broke off again. "Honestly," he said, in his most honest, public-information officer's voice, "I'd have to obtain clearances and confirmation of need-to-know from your department, and then I'd have to pass it on to the Army, and then—"

"Okay, fine. Do it."

"You have to supply the clearances."

"I haven't got time."

"You're asking me on an open line to define a hot new weapons system and break its code and you haven't got—"

"Look," Graves said. "If I call Phelps, can he call you and requisition this information?"

"*Verbal* requisition?" Morrison seemed shocked. "This is pretty heavy stuff for a verbal. You sure you don't want specifications on the ABM sites while you're at it, and maybe Polaris submarine coordinates? Any other minor details?"

Graves suppressed his anger. Morrison was such a bureaucratic ass. "I need the information," he repeated. "I need it now."

"Sounds like this may be a matter for Defense to look into,"

Morrison said. "We'd be curious to know how you got that coding in the first place. Why don't you forward us a complete report along with a requisition AB-212; that's the green form. I may be able to release the data to you in a day or so, and—"

Graves hung up.

"This is Graves."

"I know who it is," Phelps said. "What do you have to say for yourself?"

"Binary 75 slash 76," Graves said. "It's a coding—I need to know what it means."

"Binary 75 slash 76," Phelps said. There was a long pause; faintly, Graves could hear him writing it down. Finally he said, "Are you going to tell me where you came across it?"

"It's what Drew tapped from the system," Graves said.

"Oh," Phelps said.

"But Drew doesn't know what it means, either."

"How did he happen to tap in?"

"Wright told him to."

"Well, did you ask Wright why?"

"No."

"Why not?"

"I haven't picked him up yet," Graves said.

"You haven't picked him up yet."

"That's right."

"What are you waiting for, a divine edict?"

"I thought I already had that," Graves said. "But the situation is complicated. You see, Wright asked for more information from the data banks."

"More information?"

"About a State Department intelligence officer named John Graves. He pulled my file."

"Don't be an ass," Phelps said. "Pick him up immediately. He's on to you, that's clear."

"Not only is he on to me," Graves said, "he's showing me a puzzle and daring me to work it out."

"This is not a fucking poker game," Phelps said. "We can convict Wright on the basis of evidence we already have, and—"

"You can't touch him," Graves said. "When he cools down, Drew won't testify against him. You haven't got a prayer of making a case against Wright. Our only chance is to wait— and to get me my own file contents."

"You're joking."

"I'm not."

"It's out of the question."

"I want to know what he knows."

"About yourself?"

"Yes. Especially psychological test scores."

"Out of the question. Unheard of."

"You've got to do this for me," Graves said. "You've got to get me that file."

"I can't requisition it," Phelps said, "without higher authority. You know that. You're much better off picking Wright up."

"Not yet."

"I have to go to lunch," Phelps said. "Call me later. I think you're acting like a fool."

And Phelps hung up.

"State Department." A singsong voice.

"Office of the Secretary, please."

"Thank you." Lilting.

"Secretary of State, can we help you?"

"Mr. Burnett, please." Burnett was one of the Secretary's advisers. Although young, he had worked himself up from a speech writer to a close and influential position. Graves knew him slightly.

"Mr. Burnett has gone to lunch and is not back yet. He is expected shortly."

"Did he leave a number?"

"No, I'm sorry—just a moment, he's coming through the door. Whom shall I say is calling?"

"John Graves. State Intelligence."

"One moment please, Mr. Graves."

There was a very long wait, and a humming sound as Graves was put on hold. Then a click.

"Burnett here."

"Tom, this is John Graves calling."

"How are you, John? It's been a long time. When was it? Senator Evans's party, I think. You had a very cute—"

"Listen, Tom. I have a problem. I need your help."

"I'll do what I can." Said very smoothly, in the manner that all those people adopted sooner or later. No promises, but very smooth.

Graves paused. "I need my file."

"Your file?"

"Yes. My Department file."

"I don't think—just a minute—no, please hold that, I'll call him right back—John?"

"I'm here."

"I'll have to call him right back. Yes, in a few minutes. Absolutely. Five minutes, tell him five minutes. John?"

"I'm here," Graves said again.

"Now what was it? Your file?"

"Yes. I need my own file."

"I've never heard of anyone *needing* their own file," Burnett chuckled. "Curiosity, yes, but—"

"Tom. Stop being polite. This is Department business and it's very important."

"Perhaps you could stop by the office and—"

"I can't stop by the office. I'm not in Washington. I'm in San Diego."

"Oh?" There was hesitation now, the smoothness gone. "San Diego?"

"I'm doing an SS here. A guy named John Wright. I need my own—"

"Who?"

"John Wright."

"Well why didn't you say so before? I'll get it to you right away. The Secretary has directed everyone to cooperate fully with the San Diego operation."

Graves sighed. That was refreshing. He had an enormous sense of relief. What was that joke? It felt so good when he stopped.

"Let's see," Burnett said. "I'll have to get an authorization. I can do that with the Undersecretary; I don't have to bother the boss. Then we have to get it to you. You don't have access to a photoprinter?"

"No."

"Well, let's see…I don't know what sort of facilities are available in San Diego. Look. There's one sure bet. The police department. They have a printer for sure. I can transmit the file contents to you over that. But it'll take time to do the whole thing."

"I don't want the whole thing. I just want the psychological test scores."

"You do?"

"That's right," Graves said.

"Well," Burnett said, "I can have that for you right away. They'll transmit in fifteen or twenty minutes. Okay?"

"Okay," Graves said. "And thanks."

"For Christ's sake, don't mention it," Burnett said.

Graves hung up.

Downstairs in the car, Lewis said, "You look like you've gargled with Drano."

"I have," Graves said. He got into the car. "We're going to the police station."

Lewis pulled out into traffic. "Anything interesting happening upstairs?"

"They've found that Wright is preoccupied with weather today."

"Weather?"

"Yes."

"I don't get it," Lewis said.

"Neither do I," Graves said.

San Diego: 12 noon PDT

Hour 5

"You're very quiet," Lewis said, as they drove to the police headquarters.

Graves nodded. "I was thinking of an old story. It's back in the soft-data section of Wright's file. You know about the Murdock killing?"

Lewis shook his head.

"It happened in New York five years ago. Wright was married to a girl named Sarah Layne, and when it broke up, she started seeing a man named Murdock. A Texas oilman. Big spender, big ladies' man."

Lewis nodded.

"Well, Murdock got an anonymous tip that he would be killed. Got it about seven in the morning. He believed it, so he called his chauffeur and had him go over the car carefully. The chauffeur found a bomb, and notified Murdock. Murdock went down to the garage to see the bomb and had his chauffeur remove it. The chauffeur carried it away. And Murdock, who was an oilman and interested in explosives, leaned into the engine compartment to examine how the bomb had been wired in. And thirty seconds after the first bomb was removed, a second one exploded. Murdock was killed instantly."

"Nice."

"Wright was questioned but never charged. There was nothing to point to him. That's the story. But whoever did it knew a lot about Murdock."

"You think that's the way Wright operates?"

"I know it is."

Lewis was silent for a moment. "Why are we going to the police station?"

"To find out how much Wright knows about me," Graves said.

The spinning drum produced the transmitted image with almost painful slowness. It made a loud, distracting, clanking sound. Nevertheless, when the first sheet came off the drum Graves grabbed it up eagerly and read with intense concentration—ignoring the clanking, the room, the cops all around, Lewis, everything.

The first sheet was printed out in block letters, as Wright's file had been:

PSYCHOLOGICAL TESTING: JOHN NORMAN GRAVES
(STATE INT: DOM)
REASON FOR TEST: FIVE YEAR SURVEY
AUTHORIZATION FOR TEST: D/STATE 784-334-404

SPECIAL CONSIDERATIONS: QUERY SUITABILITY
FOR DOMESTIC WORK
TEST SCORES AND RESULTS:

1. RORSCHACH INK BLOT
   A. TEST SCORES: OF CHIEF INTEREST IS THE
USE OF COLOR AS RESPONSE DETERMINANT. THIS
IS CONFUSING. ON THE ONE HAND, SUBJECT USES
COLOR AS A MAJOR FACTOR IN DETERMINING
WHAT HE SEES IN THE FORM. THIS SUGGESTS
EMOTIONAL VOLATILITY AND IMPULSIVENESS.
ON THE OTHER HAND, HE IS RESPECTFUL OF
THE FORMS OF THE COLOR, SUGGESTING
CAUTION AND PERHAPS OVERCOMPLIANCE.
   B. DYNAMIC CONTENT: THERE IS A HEAVY
EMPHASIS ON THEMES OF MASCULINE

AGGRESSION. WAR, ANIMALS FIGHTING, WEAPONS, AND BLOOD RECUR OFTEN. A SENSE OF COMPETITION AND STRUGGLE IS USUALLY PRESENT. THERE IS A REMARKABLE LACK OF GUILT EXPRESSED IN ASSOCIATION WITH THESE THEMES. SUBJECT IS APPARENTLY COMFORTABLE IN SITUATIONS OF TENSION AND COMPETITION.

C. PATTERNS OF THOUGHT ORGANIZATION: NO MAJOR INSIGHTS HERE EXCEPT A STRONG SENSE OF EXCITEMENT RELATING TO ALL COMPETITIVE THEMES AND SUBJECTS.

D. TEST BEHAVIOR: SUBJECT CLEARLY REGARDS THIS TESTING SITUATION AS ONE IN WHICH HE MUST PROVE HIMSELF. IN LINE WITH HIS COMPETITIVE IMPULSES, HE DEFINITELY PLAYS OFF THE TESTER IN A RATHER UNUSUAL MANNER. HE DOES NOT TRY TO PLEASE THE TESTER OR WIN HIS APPROVAL. NOR DOES HE EVIDENCE HESITANCY OR UNCERTAINTY ABOUT HIS CHOSEN ANSWERS. INSTEAD, HE UTILIZES THE TESTER AS A SOURCE OF INSIDE INFORMATION ABOUT THE TEST ITSELF. HE ATTEMPTS TO MANIPULATE THE TESTER. ONE HAS THE SENSE THAT HE BRINGS ALL POSSIBLE RESOURCES TO ANY TEST SITUATION—AND HE REGARDS THE TESTER AS ONE AVAILABLE RESOURCE. THIS IS NOT STRICTLY FAIR, OF COURSE. BUT THERE IS A CERTAIN AMORAL QUALITY ABOUT THE SUBJECT IN COMPETITIVE SITUATIONS. ONE FEELS HE WILL DO ANYTHING TO WIN.

2. THEMATIC APPERCEPTION TEST (TAT) COMPETITION, THE NEED FOR ACTION, THE EXCITEMENT OF STRESS, AND THE HORROR OF

FAILURE IN COMPETITIVE ACTIVITY WERE
FREQUENT THEMES. IN CERTAIN INSTANCES
THERE WAS A SENSE OF IMMORTALITY ACHIEVED
BY VIGOROUS COMPETITION: THE SUBJECT
TALKED ABOUT ONE PICTURE AS SHOWING A
MAN WHO HAD "CHEATED DEATH." IT IS WORTH
INDICATING THAT IN MOST AREAS THE SUBJECT
HAS A STRONGLY DEVELOPED SENSE OF
CONVENTIONAL MORALS, PERHAPS EVEN AN
OVERRESTRICTED SENSE. HOWEVER,

"Where's the next page?" Graves said impatiently.

"Coming off now," Lewis said, and pulled it from the
machine. He handed it to Graves.

IN COMPETITIVE SITUATIONS THESE MORALITIES
ARE ABANDONED, AND IF THERE IS A CONFLICT—
SUCH AS TWO MEN COMPETING FOR THE FAVORS
OF ONE WOMAN—THE SUBJECT WILL
CHEERFULLY PROPOSE CHEATING IN ORDER TO
WIN THE DAY.

PSYCHOGENETICALLY IT IS CLEAR THE SUBJECT IS
COMPETING WITH HIS FATHER IN A CLASSIC
OEDIPAL SITUATION. STORIES ABOUT THE FATHER
EMPHASIZE THE DEMANDING, UNCOMPROMISING,
AND COMPETITIVE QUALITY OF THE FATHER-
FIGURE AND THE DIFFICULTY OF WINNING
APPROVAL. IT IS LIKELY THAT THE SUBJECT LIVES
IN A WORLD PEOPLED BY HIS FATHER, AGAINST
WHOM HE MUST CONSTANTLY STRIVE AND
COMPETE.

FAILURE IS ABHORRENT TO THE SUBJECT. HE
USUALLY DOES NOT ALLOW THAT IT MIGHT

OCCUR. PSYCHICALLY HE EQUATES FAILURE WITH
CASTRATION. THE FEAR OF FAILURE IS SO GREAT
THAT THE SUBJECT MAY BE IMPULSIVE.
QUICKNESS OF RESPONSE IS IMPORTANT TO HIM,
AND A SOURCE OF PRIDE.

3. ABBREVIATED WAIS I.Q. TEST
RAPIDITY OF RESPONSE WAS A MAJOR FACTOR
HERE IN PRODUCING AN INITIAL TEST SCORE OF
121. THE SUBJECT FELT COMPELLED TO FINISH
EACH SECTION IN LESS THAN THE ALLOTTED
TIME. TESTER'S IMPRESSION IS THAT THE SUBJECT
HAS A TEST SCORE AT LEAST 10 POINTS HIGHER
THAN THAT. THIS IS CONFIRMED BY PAST I.Q.
TESTS, WHICH HAVE SCORED THE SUBJECT IN THE
130–140 RANGE. THE SUBJECT'S WILLINGNESS TO
DAMAGE HIS OWN PERFORMANCE BY OVERLY
FAST REACTION SHOULD BE NOTED.

4. CRONBERG DIAGNOSTIC PERSONALITY
QUESTIONNAIRE:
SUBJECT SCORES HIGHLY IN MANIC SCALES WITH
SOME CONSISTENT EVIDENCE OF PARANOIA. THIS
MAY WELL RELATE TO HIS COMPETITIVE DRIVES.

5. SUMMARY

"Is there another sheet?" Graves asked.

"It's coming, it's coming," Lewis said. He smiled. "You're
really devouring this, aren't you."

"I think it's important."

"Don't you know it all already? It's about you."

"No," Graves said. "It's what somebody else thinks of me.
There's a difference."

Lewis shrugged. The third and final sheet came from the printer. Graves read it.

IN SUMMARY WE CAN SAY THAT JOHN GRAVES IS A HIGHLY INTELLIGENT, IMAGINATIVE, AND CONVENTIONALLY MORAL MAN WITH AN ASTOUNDINGLY STRONG COMPETITIVE DRIVE. HIS NEED TO COMPETE IS ALMOST HIS MOST OUTSTANDING TRAIT. IT SEEMS TO OVERWHELM EVERY OTHER ASPECT OF HIS PERSONALITY. IT IS HIGHLY DEVELOPED, AND RUTHLESS IN THE EXTREME. THERE IS NO QUESTION THAT HE IS A GOOD BETTOR, GAMBLER, POKER AND CHESS PLAYER—TO NAME HOBBIES HE PROFESSES TO LIKE.

IF THERE ARE ANY DEFECTS OR HIDDEN FLAWS IN HIS BEHAVIOR, THEY ARE HIS IMPULSIVENESS AND HIS DESIRE TO FINISH A TEST SITUATION RAPIDLY. HE FREQUENTLY PERFORMS BELOW HIS MAXIMUM LEVEL BECAUSE OF A DESIRE FOR SPEED. HE OFTEN FEELS THAT A PROBLEM IS SOLVED WHEN IT IS ONLY HALF FINISHED, OR TWO-THIRDS FINISHED. THIS SITUATION MUST BE GUARDED AGAINST BY HAVING A LESS BRILLIANT BUT MORE THOROUGH PERSON CHECKING HIS WORK AT INTERVALS.

Graves stared at the last page. "Is that all?"

Lewis nodded at the photoprinter, which had turned itself off, the roller no longer spinning. "Looks like it."

"I'll be damned," Graves said. He folded the sheets carefully, put them in his pocket, and left the police station.

✿

The radio crackled. "701, this is 702. We are following the limo east on Route Five."

Graves picked up the microphone. "Who's in the limo?"

"Only the subject, 701. And the chauffeur."

"Nobody else?"

"No, 701."

"When did they leave the apartment?"

"About five minutes ago."

"All right, 702. Out."

Graves looked at Lewis. "Where now?" Lewis asked.

"Route Five, east," Graves said. "And step on it."

The White Grumman Gulf Stream jet landed gracefully and taxied to a stop near a small hangar. The side door went down and two men climbed off. Several workmen in coveralls boarded the plane. After a moment they began unloading two large cardboard boxes.

Standing near the end of the runway of the small private field in El Cajon, Graves squinted through binoculars. The heat made everything shimmer; San Diego was hot, but El Cajon, twelve miles inland, was much hotter. "Can you make it out?" Graves asked.

Beside him Lewis leaned against the roof of the sedan to steady his arms as he held the binoculars. He pulled his elbows up quickly. "Ouch," he said. He held the binoculars freehand. "I don't know what they are," he said. "But I know what they look like. They look like mattress boxes."

Graves lowered his glasses. "That's what they look like to me. Where did this flight originate?"

"Salt Lake. A private airfield."

"Mattresses from Utah? Did the plane make intermediate stops?"

Lewis shook his head. "I don't know. But it certainly wouldn't have to stop: it's got a cruising range of just under four thousand miles."

While they watched, they heard the tinny sound of the car radio saying, "The President is due to arrive at any moment. The delegates are tense with anticipation. No one yet knows what he intends—"

Graves reached in and clicked it off.

Meanwhile, the workmen carried the two mattress-sized boxes into a green hangar.

"He rented that hangar last week," Lewis said. "Moved a lot of equipment in."

"What kind of equipment?"

"Nobody's had a look yet."

Graves bit his lip. That was an opportunity they'd missed. Several days ago somebody should have been in that hangar at midnight, taking pictures.

"Do you want to move in on him now?" Lewis asked.

Graves shook his head. "He's got five or six workmen there. There's two of us, and two in 702. None of us have guns." He sighed. "Besides, what if they really are mattresses?"

"They can't be."

Graves didn't think it possible either. But he wasn't willing to take a chance. He found himself worrying about Wright's new apartment in San Diego. Perhaps this was all a diversion, a feint to get him away from the apartment while something important was done there. He had no confidence in the men sitting across the street, observing and filming. Like every organization in the world, the State Department hired mundane men to carry out mundane jobs. Stationary surveillance was the most mundane. If the men weren't dull when they started, they soon became that way.

"We'll wait," he said.

The mattresses were taken into the hangar, and the limousine was driven inside. The doors were closed.

"Time?"

"Twelve forty-one," Lewis said.

A minute passed, and then something remarkable happened. The men came out of the hangar and walked over to the airplane. They stood alongside it, ostensibly checking it over but actually doing nothing at all; just waiting.

Wright was not among them.

"I don't get it," Graves said. "Where's Wright?"

"He must still be inside."

Their sedan was parked more than 200 yards from the hangar. But the wind was blowing in their direction, and they heard a faint mechanical sound. A kind of thumping or chugging.

Lewis opened the trunk and took out a directional microphone. It looked like a miniature radar antenna—a dish two feet in diameter, with a central barrel protruding. He put on earphones and tuned in the microphone.

"What are you getting?"

Lewis shifted the direction of the mike slightly. It was quite sensitive, but had to be aimed precisely.

"Wind."

"Can you get that noi—"

"Here."

He gave Graves the earphones. Graves listened. With the microphone aimed directly, the mechanical sound was clear. It consisted of a low hum with an intermittent pulsing thump.

"Sounds like a pump to me," he said. He listened to the sound for several seconds more. "What do you make of it?"

"A pump," Lewis said, glancing at his watch. "It's been going five minutes now."

Graves turned from the hangar to the airplane and the men who were clustered around it. They had broken up into small groups of two and three, talking quietly, occasionally glancing at the hangar. George, the chauffeur, was among them. Several of the workmen asked George questions. George kept shaking his head.

Graves set down his binoculars. Why would you clear everybody out of the hangar? He could think of only one reason: Wright didn't want them to see what was going on. But as he thought about it, he saw a second reason: that Wright was engaged in something very dangerous and wanted the others a safe distance away.

Dangerous how? Radiation? Explosives? What?

"Ten minutes now," Lewis said.

Graves scratched his head. He lit a cigarette and stared at the others by the airplane. It didn't make sense, he thought. Whatever Wright intended, it didn't make sense. If he didn't want the workmen around, he could easily have timed it so that they would be out to lunch. Instead he'd aroused their curiosity. They'd talk about this episode for days, maybe weeks afterward.

Apparently Wright didn't care about that. Why not? And then as he watched, the workmen began walking back to the hangar. He had seen no signal, but they all moved at once.

Lewis took off the earphones. "Fifteen minutes," he said. "The pump's stopped."

Graves checked his watch. It was a few minutes before 1 P.M. He was beginning to feel tired. It had been a long day already, starting with the call from Phelps at 4 A.M. and the trip to Los Angeles.

He lit another cigarette and watched the hangar. And then things began to happen very fast. The limousine drove out and off toward the entrance to the airfield. And a second vehicle emerged from the hangar.

A moving van. It followed the limousine.

Graves got onto the intercom. "702, this is 701. You got them?"

"Got them, 701."

"Stay with them. If they split up, follow the limousine; forget the van."

"Right, 701. Are you with us?"

"No," Graves said. "We're staying here." He clicked off the microphone and said to Lewis, "I want to look inside that hangar."

El Cajon: 1 p.m. PDT

Hour 4

It took them three minutes to get to the hangar, and by that time it was deserted except for an elderly man who was cleaning up with a long broom. There were one or two workmen out by the jet, but they paid no attention as Graves and Lewis went into the hangar.

The old man waved and leaned on his broom. "You looking for Mr. Johnson?"

"Yes," Graves said.

"Just missed him," the old man said. "Left a couple minutes ago."

"Damn," Graves said. "You know where he went?"

"No idea," the old man said. "He's a strange one. I guess rich people get that way." He pointed to a corner of the room. "I mean, look at that," he said. There were several boxes stacked in the corner. "Now what am I supposed to do with that? Oh, bring in plenty of it, says Mr. Johnson. And then he doesn't touch it."

Graves looked at the boxes. "What's in them?"

"Detergent," the old man said. "Gallon jugs of detergent. He wanted ten of them. Don't ask me why—he didn't touch them."

"When did he ask for them?" Graves said. He walked over and opened one of the cardboard boxes. Inside was a jug marked KEN-ALL 7588 INDUSTRIAL GRADE DETERGENT.

"Last week. Wanted to be sure he had them."

"What's this stuff normally used for?"

The old man shrugged and continued sweeping. "This is an airfield," he said. "We use a lot of it to get grease off parts. That stuff will cut anything. Axle grease, cuts it right off."

Graves nodded.

Across the hangar Lewis was bent over. "Have a look at this," he said. He pointed to a small plastic bag on the concrete floor.

"Dozens of those around," the old man said. "All over the floor when I came in."

Graves picked up the bag, sniffed it, touched the inside surface. There was some kind of milky, oily stuff inside.

"He's been getting this place ready for a week," the old man said. "Bring in equipment, take out equipment, new stuff, old stuff. Damnedest thing you ever saw. For instance, he has this washing machine—"

"Washing machine?"

"Sure. It's still here." He pointed to the corner. "You're probably too young to remember those things."

Graves walked over to it. It was an old-fashioned hand-operated tub washing machine with two rollers mounted above for a wringer. The rollers were operated with a crank. Beyond the rollers was a long, flat tray of highly polished metal.

Graves looked at the manufacturer's label: WESTINGHOUSE. The year was 1931.

"Now what," asked the old man, "does Mr. Johnson want with an old washing machine? Huh?"

Graves began to feel nervous. For the first time all day, he felt that Wright was too far ahead of him, that the clues were too subtle, that the game was beyond him. A washing machine?

Lewis touched the roller assembly. "I guess you could squeeze out a thin strip of anything on that machine," he said, "assuming it had the right consistency. A putty kind of consistency."

Plastic bags on the floor, boxes of industrial detergent in the corner—ordered but unused—and a washing machine. Then he remembered.

"Where's the pump?"

"I don't know," Lewis said. "But it doesn't matter. Look over here." He pointed to some equipment near the washing machine. A canvas tarp was draped over it; he pulled it away.

"Spray gun and four cans of paint." He bent over. "Black, yellow, white, red."

"He was using the pump to spray paint?"

"That'd be my guess," Lewis said.

Graves looked around the room. "What'd he spray it onto?"

"Whatever it was, he took it with him. Wait a minute." Lewis was again bent over. "Have a look at this."

He moved another tarp to reveal a full rubber diving wet suit, a full face mask that covered eyes, nose, and mouth, and a small air tank—one of the three that Graves had seen Wright purchase earlier in the day.

There were also several black rubber loops of different sizes.

"Just one suit?"

"Looks like it," Lewis said. He moved the suit with his foot, spreading it flat on the floor. "Wright's size?"

"Roughly. But these black loops…"

"I count six," Lewis said. "Four little ones, one big one, and one medium."

"What the hell did he use them for?"

The old man came over and stood by them, staring down at the rubber suit. "You ask me," he said, "he's just a crazy man. Rich people get that way." He sighed. "Ten gallons of detergent. Now what am I going to do with that?"

❖

Graves was tense in the car going back to San Diego. Lewis asked him what he was thinking about and he said, "My psychological tests."

"Did they surprise you?"

"In a way." He didn't bother to explain.

Graves felt the same way about his tests that he did whenever somebody sent him a photograph of himself. The question in his mind was, Is that the way you see me? Really? It was surprising. There was nothing new, no great discovery —but the quality, the emphasis, could be unsettling.

It was no news to him that he was competitive. He'd spent enough late nights playing poker with killers—and Washington had plenty of lethal poker players, blood players who got into nothing but twenty-dollar-ante games—to know that he was fiercely competitive. He liked to win and he hated to lose. That was nothing new.

The idea of his impulsiveness was not new, either. He had recognized it in himself. But the notion that this impulsiveness could be destructive—could get in his way—that was new. He had never considered it before.

There was a second problem relating to the psychological tests: How had he managed to get them in the first place? Burnett had been reluctant until Graves mentioned something about Wright. Then Burnett couldn't move fast enough.

Why?

The car radio buzzed. Lewis answered it. "701 here."

"701, this is Central. Do you have Mr. Graves there?"

"He's with me," Lewis said, and handed the mike to Graves. "Graves speaking."

"We have a Washington call for you. Hold on please."

There was a clicking, an electronic tone, and more clicking.

"Listen, you son of a bitch, I want your information." Graves recognized the voice as Morrison at Defense.

"What information?" He glanced at Lewis and lit a cigarette.

"Look, god damn it, we had a shipment stolen last night."

"Did you." Graves kept his voice calm, but his heart was thumping wildly.

"Yes we did, and now somebody's got themselves a half-ton of ZV gas in binary aerosol cylinders, and we want to know who."

"You certainly ought to be concerned," Graves said, "but this is an open line."

"Screw the open—"

"You say it was ZV gas?" Graves said.

"You're fucking right."

"Isn't that nerve gas?"

"You get your—"

"I'll tell you what," Graves said. "You fill out requisition form KL-915 and send it over to us, and maybe we can get you the information by the end of the week."

When he hung up, he began to feel better. The pieces were beginning to fall together. Wright was no longer so far ahead.

"Was he serious?" Lewis asked.

"Completely," Graves said.

"Half a ton of nerve gas was stolen?"

"Right," Graves said.

The radio buzzed again. Graves answered it.

"Where are you? This is Phelps."

"I know who it is. I'm going west on Route Five from El Cajon."

"Do you have Wright with you?"

"No."

"You've made a terrible mistake," Phelps said. "Binary 75 slash 76 is—"

"I know what it is," Graves said.

"I doubt that," Phelps said. "I'm at the Westgate Plaza Hotel, Room 1012. How fast can you get here?"

"Fifteen minutes."

"Be here in ten," Phelps said. "I have somebody you better meet."

"Is it Wright?" Graves asked.

But Phelps had already hung up.

The Westgate Plaza was one of the three greatest hotels in the world, if you believed *Esquire* magazine. If you didn't, it was a pretentious modern dump decorated with a lot of phony statuary in the lobby and downstairs lounge. Walking past statues of winged Mercury and Diana hunting, Graves took the elevator to Room 1012.

Phelps answered the door and said, "The poker game is over. I just ordered them to arrest Wright."

Graves said, "May I come in?" He was not really concerned. He knew the limousine and the furniture van were still en route back to the city. There was time to countermand the order.

"Come in," Phelps said. As Graves entered, he said, "This is Dr. Nordmann from UCSD."

Graves had never seen Nordmann before, though he knew who he was. He was a biologist on the faculty of the University of California at San Diego, and he was on the President's Advisory Council on something or other. And he was a strongly vocal opponent of chemical and biological weapons. He had been influential in getting Nixon to disavow biologicals in November 1970. He was reportedly still pushing for a similar disavowal on chemicals.

Nordmann was a tall and ungainly man with a sour expression. Graves wondered if it was permanent, or special for the occasion. Nordmann shook hands and said with some distaste, "Are you in State Intelligence too?"

"Yes," Graves said. "But we're not all the same."

Phelps gave him a sharp look.

"Well, I'm not very clear on the reason for this briefing," Nordmann said. "But I brought the film."

"Good," Phelps said. "There's a projector in the bedroom."

As they went into the bedroom, they passed the TV. Graves paused to watch: it was a demonstration in the Convention hall—a "spontaneous" demonstration for the President, who stood on the podium smiling, waving his arms, giving the V sign with both hands.

"There's very little time." Phelps said. Graves went into the bedroom.

Drapes and shades had been drawn and it was quite dark. Graves sat on the bed. Phelps took a chair. Nordmann stood in front of the small projection screen, which was mounted above the bedroom dresser. He said to Phelps, "Where should I begin?"

"Just give us necessary background for the film."

Nordmann nodded, looking sourer than ever. Distantly in the background they could hear the chanting of the delegates on the living room TV: "We want the President; we want the President…"

"You will be seeing," Nordmann said, "the final product of more than half a century of research in chemical warfare. The official date for the start of chemical war is April 22, 1915, when the Germans launched an attack with chlorine gas. It was a primitive business—you sat in your trench, opened a canister of gas, and hoped the wind would blow it toward the enemy. If it didn't, you were in trouble.

"A lot of improvements—if that's the word—came in the course of the First World War. Gas bombs, and better agents. Mustard gas, nitrogen mustard, and lewisite. All oily liquids that burn and blister your skin. They could kill you, too, but not very efficiently."

Nordmann paused. "Second World War: a new advance, again from the Germans. Remember, the Germans were the best chemists in the world for most of the twentieth century. In 1936 they synthesized a complex organophosphorous ester called tabun. It was a nerve gas. It would kill anybody who breathed enough of it. All later developments—sarin, soman, GB, VX, and ZV—are just refinements within this basic class of chemical compounds.

"It's called nerve gas," Nordmann said, "because it kills by interfering with transmission of nerve impulses. Nerves work electrically, but the impulses jump from nerve cell to nerve cell—across gaps called synapses—by chemical means. Nerve gases such as tabun, sarin, and ZV interfere with that jumping process. The result is difficulty in breathing, respiratory paralysis, and death. Now let's talk about potency."

Graves lit a cigarette and glanced at Phelps. Phelps was smiling, nodding his head as Nordmann talked. Faintly from the TV they heard: "He's our man, he's our man, he's our man…" And loud cheers.

"Tabun and sarin," Nordmann said, "or the American gas GB, must be inhaled to kill. Therefore gas masks provide an adequate defense. These gases are also relatively weak. They're not produced any more. But there is another family of gases, like VX, which can kill by absorption through the skin as well as by inhalation. The smallest fraction of an ounce is lethal. Am I clear?"

"You're clear," Graves said.

"VX is terribly powerful," Nordmann said. "The lethal

dose is estimated to be between two and ten milligrams, or a few thousandths of an ounce. But powerful as that is, it's nothing compared to ZV. ZV, like VX, is an oil. It's sticky, it clings to things, it hangs around the environment. But a tenth of a milligram is a lethal dose. In other words, it's about a hundred times as powerful as VX. We're now talking about extraordinary potency."

Phelps was still smiling, still nodding. Graves felt very cold.

"It is so potent that it has never been manufactured as a single gas. Instead it's a binary—that is, it's produced as two separate gases, each harmless by itself. But when they mix, they're deadly. The gases are designated Binary 75 and Binary 76 respectively. They're generally stored in yellow and black tanks. The film you are going to see is a French army training film showing the effects of ZV on a condemned prisoner."

Phelps got up and turned on the projector.

On the screen they saw a man in denim clothing standing in an enclosed room. The man was looking around nervously.

"This subject," Nordmann said, "is going to be exposed to the LD500 dose of the gas, that is, five-tenths of a milligram. It is a fully lethal dose."

Faintly from the other room they heard, "My fellow Americans, it is with great pleasure that I—"

At the bottom of the screen appeared the words GAS 75 INTRODUCED. The prisoner did not react. Moments later: GAS 76 INTRODUCED. The prisoner responded instantly. He placed his hand on his chest, coughed, and wiped his nose.

"—join you in this great tradition, this reaffirmation of the democratic process—"

On the screen: EARLY STAGES—RUNNING NOSE, CHEST TIGHTNESS, DIMNESS OF VISION

"—and I must urge you to follow the vision of our great land, to seek the promise, to fulfill the expectations. Let me make one thing perfectly clear—"

"Will somebody shut that door?" Graves said.

On the screen the prisoner appeared in close-up. His nose was running profusely; the liquid dripped down to his shirt. His eyes were hard black dots.

PINPOINT PUPILS

A full-body shot showed the man bent over in evident pain.

MIDDLE STAGES—CRAMPS AND NAUSEA

The prisoner vomited explosively, and the caption stated unnecessarily, VOMITING.

Very faint now from the living room they heard the sound of prolonged applause.

On the screen the prisoner was clearly confused and in great pain. A dark stain appeared on his trousers.

INVOLUNTARY URINATION

The man staggered and leaned against the wall. His legs and arms twitched and jerked spastically.

STAGGERING

The prisoner looked around briefly, but his face was contorted in agony. He lost his balance and fell, twitching and jerking, to the floor. The camera panned down to follow him. From the other room the applause continued.

DROWSINESS

The man was not really awake. He lifted his head from the floor in short jerks and finally flopped down, not moving.

COMA

The camera remained on the man. His chest was still moving slightly. Then it stopped.

CESSATION OF BREATHING

A moment later.

DEATH

The screen faded to dark. And the last letters appeared. TIME FROM INTRODUCTION OF BINARY GAS TO DEATH: 1.7 MINUTES.

The film ran out. The screen was white. Phelps turned the room lights back on.

"Jesus Christ," Graves said. He lit a cigarette and noticed that his hands were shaking.

"As I said, that man received five times the minimum lethal dose," Nordmann said quietly. "Had he gotten less, he would still have died—more slowly."

"How much more slowly?"

"From tests on animals, it may take as long as an hour or two."

"That same progression?"

"The very same."

"Jesus Christ," Graves said again.

He walked back into the living room, which seemed glaringly bright. Through the windows he could look out over the downtown area of the city. He stood with his back to the television and listened to the familiar voice saying, "My fellow Americans, and my fellow Republicans, we have come to a momentous time for our nation. We face great problems, and we face great challenges. We must act now to—"

The set abruptly clicked off. Graves turned and saw that Phelps had done it. "I hope you understand now," Phelps said. "Wright has half a ton of that gas. In the San Diego area there are a million people. Plus some very distinguished visitors. We can't afford cat-and-mouse games any longer."

"I agree," Graves said, staring out at the street below. There were no trees. He wondered why they hadn't put any trees in downtown San Diego. Trees made a difference.

Behind him Phelps picked up the telephone and dialed a

number. He said, "Phelps here. I want 702." There was a pause.

Nordmann came over to stand by Graves and look down at the street. "You know," he said, "I told the Army four years ago if they kept transporting this crap all around, it was only a matter of time before somebody—"

"You have?" Phelps said into the phone. His voice was excited. "Where?"

Graves turned. Phelps was nodding, his head bobbing up and down like a mechanical bird.

"Yes, yes…yes…good work. We'll be there in five minutes." He hung up and turned to Graves. "702 followed the limousine back to Wright's old apartment house. The van split off and went somewhere else, but the limo went back to Avenue B."

"And?"

"They arrested John Wright as he stepped from his car."

Graves nodded and tried to feel the same excitement that Phelps so clearly showed. But he still had a nagging sense of defeat, as if he had cheated at the game—or had quit too early.

"Come on," Phelps said. "You can introduce him to me."

At the apartment house two men were standing up facing the wall, guarded by the men from car 702. Phelps and Graves hurried over.

One of the men was George, the chauffeur. He was muttering something under his breath. Wright was beside him, neatly dressed in his English-cut suit.

Graves said, "You can let them turn around now." He glanced at Phelps, who had a look of total triumph on his face.

George turned and looked at Graves uncomprehendingly. Then Wright turned, and it was Graves who stared.

"This isn't John Wright," he said.

"What do you mean?" Phelps demanded.

"I've never seen this man before," Graves said. "He isn't Wright."

"We checked the wallet," one of the 702 men said. "He has his identification—"

"I don't give a damn about identification," Graves said. "This man isn't John Wright."

The man in the English suit smirked slightly.

"Who the hell is he?" Phelps said.

"That," Graves said, "is the least important question we have to answer."

And he ran for his car.

San Diego: 2 p.m. PDT

Hour 3

"Take it easy," Phelps said, grabbing the door handle. Graves took the turn from B onto Third very fast, tires squealing. "For Christ's sake."

"You said it yourself," Graves said. "A million people."

"But we have him, we know the plot, we know how it's going together—"

"We may not be able to stop it," Graves said.

"Not stop it? What are you talking about?"

Graves raced down Third, weaving among the traffic. He ran the light at Laurel. Phelps made a gurgling noise.

"Wright has been ahead of us all along," Graves said. "He must have switched clothes in the airfield hangar and sent somebody else back to San Diego in the limousine. He himself went with the furniture van."

"Well, if you know where he is now—"

"I know where he is," Graves said. "But it may be too late to stop him."

"How can it be too late?" Phelps said.

Graves didn't answer. With a squeal of tires he continued uptown, then turned down the wrong way on Alameda Street. Cars honked at him; he pulled over to the curb on the wrong side, facing the wrong way, in front of a fire hydrant.

Phelps didn't complain. He didn't have time. Graves was already out of the car and running for the building opposite Wright's new apartment house. In front of Wright's building was the furniture van.

✿

All the men in the room were clustered around the cameras and binoculars at the window. Graves burst in and said, "Is Wright there?"

"I don't know," one of the men said. "We heard he was arrested, but somebody in there sure looks like—"

"Let me see."

Graves bent over a pair of binoculars. It took only a moment to confirm his worst fears. Wright was there, donning another rubber wet suit. He was pulling rubber loops onto his ankles, his wrists, his waist, and his neck. Of course! Those strips—six strips—protected the seams of his suit from gas. As he watched, Wright put on a full face mask and twisted the valve on the small yellow air tank. The other men in the room cleared out.

"What's he doing?" Phelps said, watching through another pair of binoculars.

Graves looked around Wright's room. The four sawhorses were still in position. Across them lay two cylinders, each about eight feet long. One was painted black, the other yellow. There were stenciled letters on their sides. As he watched, Wright began connecting hoses from each of the tanks to a central T valve, which joined the hoses into a common outlet. Then he turned his attention to other equipment in the room.

"Well, that's it."

Phelps said, "Let's go get him."

"You're joking," Graves said.

"Not at all," Phelps said. "We know he's there, we've seen him connect up the hoses so that he can—"

Phelps broke off and stared at Graves.

"Exactly," Graves said.

"But this is terrible!"

"It's not terrible, it's just a fact," Graves said. "There's no way we can break into that room fast enough to get control before he turns on the valves and releases the gas."

"If we go in shooting—"

"You risk puncturing the tanks."

"Well, we can't just sit here and watch," Phelps said.

Graves lit a cigarette. "At the moment there isn't much else we *can* do."

Phelps set down his binoculars. His face was twisted; the earlier look of triumph was completely gone. "Do you have another cigarette?" he said.

Graves gave him one and then went to the phone.

"Morrison here."

"This is Graves. We've found your tanks."

"Listen, you better tell us—"

"They're on Alameda Street in San Diego."

"*San Diego!*"

"I want you to get me some people from the Navy chemical corps. I don't care where you find them or what you do to get them, just have them here in an hour. Make sure some of them have gas-protective clothing. And make sure at least one of them knows a hell of a lot about this binary gas."

Graves gave him the address and hung up. He glanced over at Phelps, who was sitting in a corner.

"Has somebody notified the President?"

"Who?"

"The President of the United States," Graves said.

"I assume so."

"Let's not assume," Graves said. "Use the other phone." And he pointed to a phone near Phelps.

Graves started to dial another call.

"I don't know how to get him," Phelps said, in a plaintive voice.

"Use the prestige of your office," Graves said, and turned away.

"Dr. Nordmann's office."

"This is Mr. Graves from the State Department. I want to speak to Dr. Nordmann."

"Dr. Nordmann had a luncheon conference and is not back yet."

"When do you expect him?"

"Well, not for several hours. He has a faculty meeting at two thirty to discuss Ph.D. candidates, and—"

"Find him," Graves said, "and tell him to call me. Tell him it's about Binary 75 slash 76. Here's my number." He gave it to the secretary.

When he hung up, one of the men at the window said, "Look what he's doing now." Graves peered through the binoculars. He saw that Wright had removed his rubber suit and was now attaching wires to the floor of the room, to the ceiling, to the walls. He plugged the wires into a central metal box the size of a shoe box.

"What the hell is that box?" Graves said.

In a corner of the room, Phelps was saying, "Yes, that's right....That's what I'm telling you, yes...a half-ton of nerve gas....Of course it's not a joke..."

Graves saw Wright attach two small mechanical devices to the valves of the two tanks. Then he ran more wires back to the box. Finally he stacked a second metal unit on top of the original box and connected still more wires.

Then Wright looked at his watch.

"Well, *somebody* better get through to him," Phelps was saying. "Yes, I'm sure it's hard…"

"What time is it?" Graves said.

"Two forty."

"The gas is called ZV," Phelps was saying. "An Army shipment was stolen in Utah during the early hours this morning. He's probably already been informed…Well, god damn it, I don't care if *you* don't know anything about it. *He* does.… Yes, it's here…"

One of the men at the window said, "He must be insane."

"Of course," Graves said. "You'd have to be insane to wipe out a million people and one whole political party. But the fact is that we've really been lucky."

"Lucky?"

"Just see that he gets the *message*," Phelps said.

"Sure," Graves said. "Those Army shipments have been going on for years. They're sitting ducks. Anybody with a little money, a little intelligence, and a screw loose somewhere could arrange for a steal. Look: Richard Speck knocked off eight nurses, but he was an incompetent. Charles Whitman was an expert rifleman, and on that basis could knock off seventeen people. John Wright is highly intelligent and very wealthy. He's going to go for a million people and one American President. And thanks to the U.S. Army, he has a chance of succeeding."

"I don't see how you can blame the Army."

"You don't?" Graves asked. He watched the other apartment through the binoculars. His eyes felt the strain; his vision blurred intermittently, and he swore. Wright appeared to be fooling with the two metal boxes in the center of the floor. He had been adjusting them for a long time.

Graves wasn't sure what it all meant. It was a control or

alarm system of some kind, though—that much was clear. And if it was a control system, it required power. Power. As Graves watched, he had an idea—one possible way to beat the system that Wright was so carefully setting up. A chance, a slim chance…

"Do it," he whispered, watching Wright. "Do it, do it…"

"Do what?" Phelps asked. He was off the telephone now.

Graves did not answer. Wright had finished with the boxes. He turned some dials, made some final adjustments. Then he took the main plug in his hand.

"He's going to do it," Graves said.

And he plugged it into the wall socket. Very plainly, very clearly, he plugged it into the wall.

"He's done it."

"Done what?" Phelps said, angry now.

"He's connected his device to the apartment electricity."

"So?"

"That's a mistake," Graves said. "He should have used a battery unit."

"Why?"

"Because we can turn off the electricity in that apartment," Graves said. "Remotely."

"Oh," Phelps said. And then he smiled. "That's good thinking."

Graves said nothing. His mind raced forward in exhilarating high gear. For the first time all day, he felt that he was not only keeping abreast of Wright but actually moving a few steps ahead. It was a marvelous feeling.

"Time?"

"Two fifty-one."

And then, as he watched, Wright did something very peculiar. He placed a small white box alongside the two other metal boxes. And he closed the windows to the apartment. Then he taped the joints and seams of the windows shut.

Then he left.

"What the hell does all that mean?" somebody asked.

"I don't know," Graves said. "But I know how we can find out."

San Diego: 3 p.m. PDT

Hour 2

Wright emerged from the apartment house lobby wearing a gray suit. He carried a raincoat over his shoulder. Graves was waiting for him, along with two federal marshals carrying drawn guns.

Wright did not look surprised. He smiled and said, "Did your son like his gift, Mr. Graves?"

Before Graves could reply, one of the marshals had spun Wright around, saying gruffly, "Up against the wall hands wide stand still and you won't get hurt."

"Gentlemen," Wright said in an offended voice. He looked at Graves over his shoulder. "I don't think any of this is necessary. Mr. Graves knows what he is looking for."

"Yes, I do," Graves said. He had already noticed the raincoat. Nobody carried a raincoat in San Diego in August. It was as out of place as a Bible in a whorehouse. "But I want to know what time it leaves."

"There's only one possible flight today," Wright said. "Connections in Miami. Leaves San Diego at four thirty."

The marshal took Wright's shoulder wallet and handed it to Graves. The ticket was inside: San Diego to Los Angeles to Miami to Montego Bay, Jamaica. The ticket was made out to Mr. A. Johnson.

"May I turn around now?" Wright asked.

"Shut up," the marshal said.

"Let him turn around," Graves said.

Wright turned, rubbing the grit of the wall from his hands. He smiled at Graves. "Your move." In the smile and the slight nod of the head, Graves got a chilling sense of the profound insanity of the man. The eyes gave it away.

Wright's eyes were genuinely amused: a clever chess player teasing an inferior opponent. But this wasn't chess, not really. Not with stakes like these.

Death in 1.7 minutes, Graves thought, and he had a mental image of the prisoner twisting and writhing on the floor, liquid running from his nose in a continuous stream, vomit spewing out.

Graves realized then that he had mistaken his opponent for too long. Wright was insane. He was capable of anything. It produced a churning sensation in Graves's stomach.

"Take him inside," Graves said to the marshal. "I want to talk to him."

The three of them sat in the lobby of the apartment building. It was the kind of lobby that aspired to look like the grossest Miami Beach hotels; there were plastic palms in plastic pots and fake Louis XIV furniture which, apparently out of fear that someone would want to steal it, was bolted to the imitation marble floor. Under other circumstances the artificiality of the surroundings would have annoyed Graves, but now it somehow seemed appropriate. By implication the room suggested that falsehoods were acceptable, even preferable, to the truth.

Graves sat in a chair facing Wright. The marshal sat diagonally facing both of them and the only exit. The marshal held his gun loosely in his lap.

Wright looked at the marshal and the position of the gun. "That's what it's all about," he said, and smiled again. That insane smile.

"How do you mean?" Graves said.

Wright sighed patiently. "Do I confuse you?"

"Of course. That was your intention."

"I doubt that I've confused you much," Wright said. "You've really done very well, Mr. Graves. May I call you John?"

The condescending tone was unmistakable, but Graves merely shrugged. He glanced at his watch: 3:05.

"Very well, indeed," Wright continued. "For the last month or so, John, I've had the feeling that you were a worthy adversary. I can't tell you how reassuring that was."

"Reassuring?"

"I prefer to do things well," he said. He took a slim cigar from a gunmetal case and lit it. "I mean elegantly, with a certain finesse. In a situation like this, one needs a proper opponent. I was immensely reassured that my opponent was you, John." Wright sighed. "Of course, I have another opponent as well," he said. "One totally lacking in finesse, elegance, and grace. The sad thing is, he thinks he's a statesman."

"You mean the President?"

"I prefer to think of him," Wright said, "as that man who rode the bench for so many years. Why did he ride the bench? Did you ever think of that? The answer is simple enough— because he wasn't a good player. He was inept. He was incompetent. He was a bumbling fool."

"You feel strongly about him."

"I feel strongly about his *policies*."

"China?"

"Ten years ago," Wright said, "if I asked you the name of the American President most likely to institute wage and price controls, welfare reform, and diplomatic relations with Communist China, would you have ever thought of this man? It's *insane*, what he's doing."

"What about what you're doing?"

"Somebody has to stop him," Wright said. "It's as simple as that."

"I wouldn't call nerve gas a democratic method." Graves stared at him. "What are those metal boxes in the center of the floor upstairs?"

Wright smiled. "Enough politics, eh?" He puffed on his cigar, billowing light smoke. "Very well. Down to business." A thought seemed to occur to him. "But if I tell you, how will you know it's the truth?"

"That's my job."

"True, true. There are actually three boxes, as I'm sure you observed from your surveillance station across the street. I had to get an extension cord in order to place the boxes in clear view of the window."

"Very thoughtful."

"I felt you'd appreciate it," Wright said. "The first box is a timer. It controls a rather intricate set of staging sequences for the equipment in the room."

Graves took out a cigarette. His hands shook slightly as he lit it. He hoped Wright wouldn't notice—but that, of course, was wishful thinking. Wright would notice.

But Wright didn't comment on it. "The second box," he said, "is an impedance and vibration sensor. There are contact points located around the room. On the door, on the floor, on the walls. Any excessive vibration—for example, a man walking on the floor of the room—will set off the gas. It's a commercial unit. I bought it last week." He smiled then. "A friend made the purchase, so that you wouldn't be aware of it."

"The third box?"

"The third box is the little white unit alongside the other

boxes. It's a battery. We wouldn't want to be dependent on electricity in the apartment, after all. You could turn that off remotely."

Graves had a sinking feeling, and it must have showed, because Wright laughed. "Oh, you were planning to do that, were you?" He shook his head. "Too simple. Much too simple. I wouldn't make a mistake like *that*."

"What's the voltage of the batteries?" Graves snapped, trying to regain control of the situation.

"A very intelligent question," Wright said. "I am tempted to lie, but I won't. It is a twelve-volt unit."

"Amperage?"

"I haven't the faintest idea."

"That doesn't concern you?"

"The amperage is adequate."

"Adequate for what?"

Wright smiled. "Really," he said, "you don't expect me to hand you everything on a silver platter."

"Actually, I do."

"Then you're being naive. How do you expect to extract information from me?" He glanced at his watch. "There is not a lot of time, and although I am sure you could torture me inventively, you couldn't get me to talk. Not fast enough."

"Why did you close the apartment windows?"

Wright smiled. "Fascinating. I was wondering if you'd catch that. I taped them, too."

"Yes, you did."

"I closed the windows," Wright said, "because the mechanism in that room anticipates some action you will take."

"Some action I will take?"

"Yes."

"You're being cryptic."

"I can afford to be cryptic."

"What's the point of the scintillation counter?"

"An interesting problem, but not so interesting as the explosives."

Graves tried to keep his face blank, but it didn't work.

"Ah," Wright said. "You don't know about the explosives? There was a robbery of twenty pounds of plastic explosive—Compound C, I believe it's called—earlier today, on the freeway. A hijacked truck. I'm surprised you haven't already been informed."

Graves was beginning to sweat. He resisted the impulse to wipe his forehead. He sat back in his chair and tried to be calm.

"You seem nervous," Wright said.

"Concerned."

"There is no need to be nervous," Wright said. "I can assure you right now, it is impossible for you to get into that room alive. I don't advise you to try."

"You seem quite nonchalant."

"Oh, I am." He turned the cigar in his mouth, removed it, stared at the burning tip.

"We can hold you, of course."

"You mean, prevent me from leaving San Diego?"

"Yes."

"I'd expect that."

"You don't care?"

"Not particularly."

"But you'll die," Graves said.

"A great many people will die, in fact," Wright said, and his eyes glowed with a sudden mad intensity. "You may have noticed that weather conditions are perfect. There is an inversion layer over the city. Any released gases will be blown west—across the city—and will be trapped there. Do you know much about meteorology?"

"A little."

"You know," Wright said, "it's a funny thing about chemical agents. The military makes them, but they don't have much military use. By their very nature, they work best in high population density situations. And that means civilian populations. That's where you get the most bangs for your buck, so to speak."

His eyes literally sparkled as he talked. "But the irony goes even further," he said. "Modern city life improves the effectiveness of these weapons. You can imagine a city like San Diego as existing with a giant plastic dome over it. That's the inversion layer. It blankets the area, holds in all the automobile fumes and exhaust gases that make city air so obnoxious. That inversion layer will hold any released gas—or, in the case of ZV, oil droplet suspension."

Graves snapped his fingers. "The detergent!"

"Yes," Wright said. "Good for you. The detergent was ordered in case I had an accident in the hangar. Have to cut that oil somehow. Detergent was the best way. But," he said, "I didn't have an accident. Nothing went wrong."

At that moment Phelps stuck his head in the door. "Nordmann's here."

"All right," Graves said.

Wright looked appreciative. "Good move," he said. "Nordmann's an excellent man. In fact, it was one of his articles —detailed, scholarly, and complete—that suggested to me the possibility of stealing some gas in the first place."

Again there was that glow in Wright's eyes. Graves found himself getting angry. He stood up abruptly. "Don't let him go anywhere," he said to the marshal.

"I wouldn't think of it, until I've finished my cigar," Wright said.

Graves left the lobby.

Nordmann was outside, standing on the sidewalk with Phelps. They were both looking up, talking.

Graves said, "The gas is up there. Is there any antidote?"

"To ZV? Nothing very good."

"But there is an antidote?"

"There's a sort of theoretical antidote. If a person has a mild exposure, it may be possible to inject chemicals to block the effects of the gas."

"Can you get those chemicals?"

"Yes, but not in sufficient quantities to protect very many—"

"Get as much as you can," Graves said. "Do it immediately." He turned to Phelps. "Notify the San Diego police. Evacuate this block and cordon it off. Cordon off the blocks on both sides as well. And I mean a cordon—nobody in and nobody out." He paused. "What happened with the President?"

"He's leaving within the hour."

"For sure?"

"I assume so."

"Better check again."

Phelps nodded toward the lobby. "Is he talking?"

"He's saying what he wants to say," Graves said.

"My God, he's a cool customer."

"What did you expect?" Graves said, and went back inside. When he returned, he found the marshal smoking one of Wright's slim cigars. Graves shot him a look; the marshal quickly stubbed it out.

"Waste of a good cigar," Wright said. "Why can't we all be friends?"

Graves sat down. "What did you paint in the hangar?"

"Paint?"

"Yes We found a spray gun and several cans of paint."

"Oh, that."

"What did you paint?"

"I don't believe I'll answer that."

"What did you paint?"

"You show a certain redundancy of mind," Wright said. "It's tiresome, and disappointing. I expected you to be more clever." He was silent a moment. "I will tell you one thing," he said.

"What's that?" Graves resented the eagerness that he heard in his own voice.

"I have devised a multiple staging system. Actually, several interlocking systems. If one fails or is thwarted, another takes over. It's quite beyond you, I can assure you of that. However, I will tell you I am dependent on one external system, which is fortunately quite reliable."

"What's that?"

"You," Wright said. "Everything has been designed especially for you, so to speak."

Wright's calmness was infuriating. Graves bit his lip, trying to control his anger.

"What time is it?" Wright asked.

"Three forty," the marshal said.

"Thank you. Do you have any other questions, John?"

"One or two," Graves said. His anger was so intense that it clouded his judgment. He fought the feeling.

"I can see you're upset," Wright said. "And you haven't asked me some rather obvious questions. One is, when will the gas go off?"

Graves stared at him, almost shaking with fury.

"The answer," Wright said, "is five p.m. exactly. The gas

will go off then. It will begin to drift in a predictable way and will have blanketed the city with good saturation by about five thirty, the peak of the rush hour: maximum number of people on the streets, and so on. Now, it seems to me there was something else I wanted to tell you…"

Graves wanted to beat the man to a pulp. He wanted to smash his face, to shatter his nose, his teeth… He had a brief image of himself standing over Wright, pounding him.

"Damn," Wright said, "it was just on the tip of my tongue. Well, no matter. It couldn't have been that important." He sighed. "I think," he said, "this concludes the questions for today. I have nothing else to say."

Graves stared at him for a moment. "You don't leave us much choice."

Wright smiled. "I believe you call it 'softening up'; is that right?"

"More or less."

"An interesting notion," Wright said, "but now I must leave."

And with astonishing speed he jumped from his chair and raced for the door. The marshal crouched down and held his gun stiffly.

"Don't!" Graves shouted, and knocked the pistol away. The marshal looked stunned. "Don't shoot him!"

Wright was out the door. A second marshal stood outside. He wore a look of surprise, as Wright slammed him in the groin with one knee. He doubled over. Wright sprinted for the stairs to the basement.

"He's going for the garage," Graves said. He pushed the other marshal toward the door to the basement and then ran outside.

Phelps was directing a half-dozen marshals and policemen to cordon off the area.

"Wright's escaped!" Graves shouted. He ran down the street, looking for the underground-garage exit.

"Where?"

"The garage."

"Can he get out?"

The marshals and police all drew their guns. A single shot echoed inside the garage.

"How did this happen?" Phelps demanded.

Graves looked at the marshals and the cops standing by the ramp from the garage. "Don't shoot him," he said. "Whatever happens, don't shoot him."

There was a long silence. Nothing further was heard from inside the garage.

"I demand to know what happened," Phelps said.

Graves listened.

Nothing.

The cops looked at each other.

"Hey," a cop shouted, from the garage. "He went out the other exit!"

Graves instantly realized that he had made a mistake. Wright was too smart to think he could escape from the garage of this building; he would have another plan. Graves started to run. So did the police.

"Where'd he go?"

"Next building. Other block."

Graves sprinted down the ramp into the garage and toward the other garage exit. He ran up a short flight of stairs through an open door and came out into an alley. The alley connected with the opposite block. He ran down it, the cops following, their footsteps echoing.

They saw no one.

"Where'd he go?"

Graves held up his hand. Everyone paused. They heard

the sound of an engine. It was coming from the garage of a
building on the adjacent block.

"Where's the exit from that garage?"

Graves ran forward. The exit must be on the street. They
came out into the next street—deserted, heavily cordoned
off at each end, with a police car crosswise blocking the road,
cops standing around.

The sound of a racing engine. They saw a ramp.

"Don't sh—"

Wright's Alfa came up the ramp, moving very fast. The
cops and marshals scrambled out of the way. They fired as
they ran.

Graves felt sick.

But the Alfa was still going. It made a twisting right-hand
turn, slamming into a parked car. There were more gunshots.
The side windows shattered into great spiderwebs, but somehow the car continued, gears grinding as it raced down the
street.

Wright had planned it well, Graves thought. He would
have made his escape by sneaking through the buildings if
it hadn't been for the roadblock. He didn't expect that;
Graves himself had ordered it on the spur of the moment.

The Alfa roared down the street.

"He wasn't expecting the roadblock," Graves said. "He
didn't count on that."

"Whose side are you on?" Phelps demanded.

At the end of the street four policemen waited by the
parked patrol car. As the Alfa bore down on them, they
dropped to their knees, holding their guns stiff-armed before
them.

"Don't shoot!" Graves screamed.

The cops began to fire. The tires on the Alfa exploded.

The front windshield shattered. The car wobbled, flipped on its side, and slammed into a parked car. The horn began to blare.

Graves ran over to the Alfa and tried to open the door. It was jammed shut. He looked in through the shattered windshield and saw Wright's face, a bloody pulp, the features indistinguishable. As he watched, a tiny stream of blood spurted rhythmically from Wright's neck. Then it became a seeping red stain across his collar.

He turned away from the car.

"Is he dead?" Phelps said, running up.

"Yes," Graves said. "He's dead."

"How can we turn off that fucking horn?" Phelps said.

Graves stared at him and walked away.

San Diego: 4 p.m. PDT

Hour 1

His sense of shock was profound. Of all the alternatives, of all the possibilities and options, he had never expected this. He had never expected Wright to die.

Graves walked back up the street slowly, trying to gather his thoughts. What did he do next?

Nordmann came up to him. "That's a damned shame," he said.

"You bet it is," Graves said.

Nordmann looked at the crowd clustered around the wrecked car. "One thing, though," he said.

"What's that?"

"It proves he could make a mistake."

"It was a big one," Graves said.

"Yes," Nordmann said, in a calm, logical voice. "But it *was* a mistake."

Graves nodded and walked back toward the surveillance building. He thought about what Nordmann had said. The more he thought about it, the more encouraged he was. Because Nordmann was right.

Wright had erred. And that was encouraging.

One of the aides came running out of the building, waving Wright's ticket. "Mr. Graves," he said. "There's something very strange going on. We just checked this ticket. He canceled that reservation yesterday."

Protect me from fools, Graves thought. "Of course he did."

"Of course?"

"Look," Graves said. "He planned to let us catch him, and

he planned his escape. But he couldn't get far if we knew his real airplane reservation, could he?"

"Well, I guess not…"

"Keep checking the airlines. Check Los Angeles, too. You'll find he had a reservation somewhere."

Phelps came over. "The sniffer's arrived."

"Has it? Good." Graves walked across the street to Wright's apartment building. Phelps trailed behind him in silence.

Finally Phelps said, "I hope you know what you're doing."

Graves didn't answer. Because the fact was that he didn't know what he was doing. He knew only in a general way what Wright intended. Wright had made Graves a part of the total mechanism, and therefore Graves would have to cancel himself out—inactivate himself—by not doing what was expected of him.

In order to do that, he had to decipher as many elements of the total staging mechanism as possible. Only then could he determine how he was intended to participate in the staging sequence that controlled the final release of gas.

The sniffer was the first step in deciphering the sequence.

Graves stood outside the door to Wright's apartment. Next to him Lewis held a gunlike instrument in his hand. The gun was attached to a shoulder pack with a dial. Lewis pointed the instrument at the door and ran it along the cracks and seams.

Behind them at the far end of the hallway, six people, including Phelps, stood and watched. Graves wanted everyone away from the door so that they wouldn't accidentally trip the vibration sensors. He didn't know how sensitively they were tuned, but he wasn't taking any chances.

After a moment Lewis turned away with the instrument. "Wow," he said.

"You get a reading?"

"Yeah," he said. "High nitrogen and oxygen content, trace phosphorus."

"Meaning?"

"Plastic explosive, very near."

"Near the door?"

"Probably just on the other side," he said.

Graves said, "Is there any chance you're wrong?"

"The sniffer is never wrong," he said. "You've got oxide of nitrogen fumes, and that's explosives. You can count on it."

"All right," Graves said. He walked away from the door. He had to trust the sniffer. It had been developed for use in Vietnam and had been adapted for customs operations, smuggling, and so on. It was incredibly sensitive and incredibly accurate. If the sniffer said plastic explosive was behind the door, he had to believe it. He walked back to Phelps at the end of the hallway.

"Well?"

"There's explosive on the other side of the door."

"Nice," Phelps said. "What do we do now?"

"Try to get a better look inside the apartment," Graves said. He glanced at his watch.

"It's four ten," Phelps said. "When did your friend say it would go off?"

"Five," Graves said.

"I hope you know what you're doing," Phelps said again.

Graves sighed. He wondered if he could ever explain to Phelps that that wasn't the problem. The problem was figuring out what Wright expected him to do—and then *not* doing it.

Across the street in the surveillance room looking down on Wright's apartment, he talked to Nordmann. Nordmann had brought a cardboard box full of medical supplies—syringes, needles, bottles of liquid. He was frowning down at it. "This is the best I could manage on short notice," he said.

"Will it work?" Graves said.

"It's the standard therapy," Nordmann said. "But we haven't got much. This quantity will treat two or three people for exposure, that's all."

"Then let's make sure it doesn't come to that."

Nordmann smiled slightly. "It better not," he said. "Because you need somebody alive and well to administer it."

"Is it hard to administer?"

"Tricky," Nordmann said. "There are two different chemicals, atropine and pralidoxime. They have to be balanced."

Graves sighed. "So the antidote is a binary, too."

"In a sense. The two chemicals treat different effects of the gas. One treats the peripheral nervous system, the other the central. The chemicals are dangerous in themselves, which makes it all much harder."

"Fighting fire with fire?"

"In a sense," Nordmann said.

The two men stood staring out the window at the apartment opposite. Phelps was in a corner using a walkie-talkie. "You in position?"

A response crackled back. "In position, sir."

"Very good." Phelps clicked off the walkie-talkie. "We've got two cops stationed outside the door to that apartment," he said.

"Fine," Graves said. "Just so they don't get too close to the door."

"I have them ten feet away."

"That should be fine."

In the hallway outside Wright's apartment, Officers Martin and Jencks of the San Diego Police Department stared at the closed door and leaned against the wall.

"You understand any of this?" Jencks said.

"Nope," Martin said.

"But they said not to get too close to the door."

"That's right."

"You know why?"

"I don't know nothing," Martin said. He took out a ciga-rette. "You got a match?"

"Maybe we shouldn't smoke…"

"Who's going to know?" Martin said.

Jencks gave him a match.

Graves stood with Nordmann in the surveillance room across the street.

"Wright booby-trapped the apartment?"

"Elaborately," Graves said. "He told me some of it. I'm sure he didn't tell me everything."

"And it goes off at five?"

"Yes."

"Forty-five minutes from now," Nordmann said. "Is the Navy sending people with protective suits? Because protected people could just walk right in."

"Nobody can walk right in," Graves said. "He's wired the room with explosive. That's why we've got the guards over there."

Nordmann grimaced. "Explosive?"

"Twenty pounds of it."

The TV in the corner of the room showed the Convention. A monotonous voice was saying, "Mr. Chairman…Mr. Chair-man, we request the floor…Mr. Chairman…" There was the loud banging of a gavel.

"Turn that damned thing off," Graves said. Someone turned it off.

At the window two men grunted as they lifted a huge lens onto a heavy-duty tripod. It was screwed into place and ad-justed. "Ready, Mr. Graves."

"Thank you." Graves went to the window.

"What's that?" Nordmann said.

"A fifteen-hundred-millimeter telephoto," Graves said. "It's the best look we can get."

He peered through the giant lens. The view was so enormously magnified that at first he didn't know what he was looking at. Using a fine-knurled knob, he moved the lens and saw he was focused on a crack in the floor. He moved across the floor to the boxes. He shifted the lens upward, examining each box in detail.

"Take a look at this," he said, stepping away.

Nordmann squinted through the lens. "Three stacked boxes," he said. "I can't make out much…"

"Neither can I." Graves folded his arms across his chest and stared out the window. He tried to think logically, but he was having trouble; Wright's death had unnerved him, whether he wanted to admit it or not.

And the system seemed so complicated. Staging sequences, timers, vibration sensors, explosives…His head ached. How the hell would he unravel it?

"Let's work it backward," Nordmann said. "What's the most important element in the system?"

"The gas."

"How is it controlled?"

"There are spring-loaded valve mechanisms. They can be tripped by a solenoid."

"And they presumably have a timer of some kind."

"Presumably."

"Battery-powered or line-powered?"

"Well, he's plugged one of the boxes into the wall. But the valve mechanisms are probably battery-powered."

Nordmann nodded. "That makes sense," he said. "He wouldn't have the most important elements dependent on an external system. So what did he plug into the wall?"

"I don't know."

"Vibration sensors?"

"Maybe," Graves said. He looked at his watch. It was 4:20. He would have to move soon. What had Wright expected him to do? The psychological report was folded up in his pocket. He took it out and looked at the last few lines.

IF THERE ARE ANY DEFECTS OR HIDDEN
FLAWS IN HIS BEHAVIOR, THEY ARE HIS
IMPULSIVENESS AND HIS DESIRE TO FINISH
A TEST SITUATION RAPIDLY.

Well, he didn't have much choice now. He was going to have to make a move, and soon.

"You know," Nordmann said thoughtfully, "most of the equipment in that room is defensive. It's designed to keep people out of there until the gas is ready to be released. But I suspect some of those defenses are meant to be penetrated."

"I agree," Graves said. "And in any case, we have to start penetrating."

"Wall current first?" Nordmann asked.

Graves nodded. He glanced at Phelps, who was sitting in a corner of the room literally chewing his nails. Graves sent Lewis across the street to disconnect power to the apartment. Four minutes later, the power was off. Graves watched through the big telephoto lens. He saw a single yellow pilot light in the vibration sensor box go out.

"Well," Nordmann said, "that's a start. We've killed part of the system."

"Have we?" Graves said. He watched through the telephoto as the solenoid mechanism tripped open the tank valves, then a moment later tripped them shut.

The apartment became filled with whitish gas.

"What's happening?" Phelps said, very agitated.

"Quick," Graves said. "Those cops. Tell the cops."

"What cops?" Phelps said.

Officer Martin finished his cigarette and ground it out on the floor. His heel squeaked.

"Sssh," Jencks said, suddenly tense.

"What is it?"

"Sssssh. Listen."

The two men listened in silence. There was a hissing.

"You hear that?" Jencks said.

"Yeah. It's coming from the room."

"Are you sure?"

Martin moved closer to the door. "I think so—"

"Maybe you shouldn't—"

Martin began to cough. His nose ran. "Shit," he said. "What is this?" He coughed again.

Jencks went forward to help him. Then Jencks felt the stinging in his nostrils, and the liquid began to pour over his shirt. He didn't know a nose could run that way. His eyes ached and stung; he felt dizzy. "What the hell…" He had a coughing fit.

The walkie-talkie crackled. "This is Phelps," a voice said. "Over."

Martin took a step toward the walkie-talkie and fell to the floor. Now he could see the faint wispy whiteness seeping through the door.

"This is Phelps. Over."

Jencks was coughing loudly and groaning.

Martin stretched out his hand toward the walkie-talkie. He was weak. His arm trembled. Then, without warning, he vomited and lost consciousness.

✶

"I'm not getting an answer," Phelps said.

Graves and Nordmann exchanged glances, then looked back out the window at the opposite apartment. The room now had a faint milky haze.

"Are they dead?" Phelps said.

"Probably."

"How can you just stand there?"

"Because," Graves said, "it was just a short burst. The valves are turned off again."

Phelps looked puzzled.

"It wasn't a full release," Graves said. "It's just a partial release, to fill the room with gas. That's why Wright carefully closed the windows. Now we *really* can't get in there."

"You sound so appreciative," Phelps said.

"I'm not. But we understand now what Wright meant by a complex staging sequence."

"God damn it, this is not a jigsaw puzzle! Two cops have died and—"

"We're all right," Nordmann said quietly, "until five p.m."

"And what do you intend to do between now and then?" Phelps demanded angrily. "I'm going to call the Navy," he said. "Their men were supposed to be here an hour ago. It's four thirty now."

Graves stared at the gas-filled apartment. He had a brief mental image of the two cops staggering drunkenly in the hallway. He pushed it away; he could consider it later.

Beside him Nordmann said, "It's really quite clever."

Graves said, "How thick is the gas in that room?"

"Hard to say," Nordmann said. "The normal color of the gas is white. I don't think the density is very great. Why?"

"If you shot me full of those antidotes, could I survive the atmosphere in that room?"

"I don't know."

"Would I have a chance?"

"A chance? Of course. But even if you could survive, how would you get in? You said yourself it's wired with explosives. You can't go in the front door."

"I wasn't thinking of the door," Graves said. "I was thinking of the window."

"The window?" Nordmann frowned. "I don't know…"

Graves looked down at the street below, where an ambulance had pulled alongside the wrecked Alfa. A half-dozen cops and orderlies were trying to open the door, but it was still jammed shut. "Damn," he said. "I wish he were still alive."

"It probably wouldn't matter," Nordmann said absently. He was staring across at the other building.

Graves said, "How good are my chances with the antidote?"

"Four thirty-five," somebody said.

"Maybe one in two," Nordmann said. "At best."

"All right. Let's do it."

"Are you sure?"

"What choice do I have?"

Nordmann considered this, then nodded. "Sit down," he said. "I'll fix a syringe."

He quickly filled a syringe with two solutions, one pale yellow, the other clear.

Graves sat and watched him. "How do I take it?"

"Intravenously."

"You mean, in the vein?"

"Yes."

"I can't possibly shoot into my veins."

"You can," Nordmann said, "if I tape on an IV line. Roll up your sleeve."

Graves rolled up his sleeve, and Nordmann tied a rubber tourniquet around his arm. He slapped the veins to make them stand out. Then he turned back to the syringe. "I hope I've got this mixture right," he said. He tapped the bubbles of air out of the syringe.

"So do I," Graves said.

Nordmann attached the syringe to a piece of flexible plastic tubing. At the end of the tubing was a needle. "I'll put the needle into your vein," he said, "and tape the syringe to your arm. Just before you enter the room, you can inject the contents."

Graves felt the coldness of alcohol on his forearm, and then the prick of the needle.

"Don't move," Nordmann said. "Let me tape it down." He removed the tourniquet, applied the tape, and stepped back. "Done."

Graves looked at the equipment taped to his arm. "You sure this will work?"

"I told you the odds," Nordmann said.

Graves stood up. "Okay," he said. "Time?"

"Four thirty-nine."

"Let's go," he said, and ran for the elevator.

They came to the street and ran outside. By his side Nordmann was puffing, red in the face. Graves felt no strain at all; he was tense and full of energy. "Rope," he shouted to a cop. "We need rope."

The cop went off to get some.

"Hurry!"

The cop hurried.

Graves looked at Nordmann. "Listen," he said. "I just had a thought. The gas leaked out of the nineteenth floor and killed those two cops. Right?"

"Right."

"What's to prevent us from getting knocked off in the elevator as we go up to the twentieth floor?"

"Nothing," Nordmann said. "It's a risk we have to take. If enough gas has leaked back into the building, we may die on our way up."

"Is that all you have to say?"

Nordmann shrugged. "That's the situation."

Two burly cops came over. One had a coil of white nylon rope over his shoulder. "Come with us," Graves said. And he ran with Nordmann into the apartment building.

The elevator creaked up slowly. Graves fidgeted. Nordmann seemed very calm. The two cops looked at each other, obviously not understanding what was going on. They stared suspiciously at the syringe taped to Graves's arm.

They passed the tenth floor.

"Listen," Graves said. "I had another thought. ZV is an oil, right?"

"Yes."

"Well, when I get into that room, all the surfaces will be coated with oil. And deadly. Right?"

"Probably not," Nordmann said. "It takes time for the droplets to settle. If the room is cleared of gas fast enough, the surfaces should be safe."

"You sure?"

"I'm not sure about anything."

They passed the fifteenth floor. Graves resisted the impulse to hold his breath. He looked at Nordmann. Nordmann crossed his fingers.

Seventeenth floor. Eighteenth floor. Nineteenth floor. Graves waited for the gas to hit him, but nothing happened. They came to the twentieth, and the doors opened.

"We made it," he said.

"So far," Nordmann said.

They hurried down the corridor.

"Time?"

"Four forty-two," one of the cops said.

They came to Apartment 2011, the one directly above Wright's. The building had been evacuated and the door was locked. The two policemen threw themselves at the door. It didn't move. They tried again without success.

Nordmann went hurrying down the hallway and returned with a fire axe. He swung once at the door. The axe barely bit into the wood.

"Let me do that," one of the cops said, and swung hard near the lock.

"Knock it down, knock it down," Graves said.

It took time. There was no easy crash and splintering; the wood was new and strong and thick. Finally the cop managed to bash a hole large enough to admit his hand. He reached in and turned the lock. The door swung open, and they came into an apartment that was all chintz and doilies and heavy furniture.

Graves went directly to the window and flung it open. He looked out and down, feeling the hot, gusty August wind. He was sweating hard.

One of the cops tied the nylon rope around his waist.

"Tell me what I do," Graves said to Nordmann, and pointed to the syringe.

"Okay," Nordmann said. "You press that syringe to give yourself an injection of the antidote. You can push the plunger this far—" he touched the side of the syringe "—and be safe. More than that, and you will suffer effects similar to the gas itself. Clear?"

"Christ," Graves said.

The cop cinched the rope tight around his waist.

"Remember," Nordmann said, "that you're counteracting the effects of the gas and you must pay out antidote in relation to your exposure to the toxin. Clear?"

"What happens if I undershoot?"

"That's worse than overshooting. It's better to give yourself too much than too little. But not too much too much."

"When do I begin to inject?"

"Just before your exposure to the gas. If you're exposed before injecting, you'll have only five or ten seconds of clear consciousness. So do it before."

"Four forty-five," one of the cops said.

Graves swung one leg over the window ledge.

"You afraid of heights?" Nordmann asked.

"Terrified," Graves said.

"Good luck," Nordmann said as Graves crawled completely over the sill and hung there for a moment with his hands.

"We've got you," one of the cops said.

Graves let go and began his descent down the face of the building.

He tried to balance himself against the stone wall. It was remarkable how dirty the outside of an apartment building could be. His fingers scraped over a crust of dirt and grime and pigeon droppings. He tried not to look down, but once he lost his balance and twisted upside-down, so that he was descending head first. He stared straight at the ground.

The people were minute below him. He was vaguely aware of the hot wind whistling in his ears; it was the only sound he heard. He seemed completely isolated, completely alone. He reached for the stones of the apartment wall with tense fingers. He slowly pulled himself around until he was upright again.

His descent continued more slowly. He checked his watch. It was 4:47. Plenty of time, plenty of time...

He was now just above Wright's window. He could see the interior of the apartment clearly—the two tanks, yellow and black, the connecting hoses, the equipment, the snaking cables and electrical lines.

"Okay," Nordmann shouted. "Inject yourself!"

Graves hung dangling and twisting on the rope, nineteen floors above the street, and tried to grab his own forearm. He was clumsy; his breath came in hissing gasps; the rope was tight around his ribs. Finally he got the syringe and pushed the plunger partway down.

"Go!" Nordmann shouted.

Graves kicked away from the wall, swinging out into space, and came back with his legs stiffly extended. The glass smashed under his feet, and he was swung smoothly, almost easily, into the apartment.

He dropped to the floor, coughed, and got to his feet. Immediately the acrid piercing sting of the gas invaded his nostrils and brought tears to his eyes. He felt lightheaded. *The antidote isn't working,* he thought, and fell to his knees. He was gasping for breath. He looked up at the equipment, the tanks above him.

He was very dizzy. He injected more antidote. And then suddenly he was all right. His mouth was dry and he was still light-headed, but he was all right. He got to his feet and moved toward the tanks. At every moment he expected to hear the ominous hiss and sizzle of the releasing gas, but it never came. He stood in the center of the room, with the wires and cords all across the floor at his feet and the white gas drifting gently out the broken window.

He disengaged the first valve mechanism, unhooking the solenoid trip wire. Then the other mechanism. And then he sighed.

It was done.

The mechanism could not release the gas; the tanks were isolated. He relaxed, blinked his aching eyes, swallowed dryly, and checked his watch. 4:49. It hadn't even been close.

"Graves!"

That was Nordmann, shouting to him from the floor above. Graves went to the window and looked up.

"You all right?"

Graves tried to talk, but a hoarse, dry croak came out. He nodded and waved instead.

"Can't talk?"

Graves shook his head.

"That's the effect of the antidote," Nordmann said. "You'll be okay. We want to come down. Can you open that door for us?"

Graves nodded.

"Okay. We'll come down."

Graves opened all the other windows in the apartment, then went back to the center of the room and crouched over the three metal boxes. One was a timer; one was a battery; the third, when he turned it over, was a hollow shell, empty inside. He stared at it and shook his head. Another diversion —but it didn't matter now.

He went to the door and looked closely at the vibration sensors. They were just rubber suction cups from a toy bow-and-arrow set, with some wires attached. Totally phony. He sighed.

Nordmann called from the other side of the door. "Graves? You there?"

Graves let him in. He had a glimpse of two San Diego cops sprawled on the floor in the hallway as Nordmann came into the room. "Gas is dissipated now, but those poor bastards got it full. How do you feel?"

Graves nodded, smiled.

"Dry mouth?"

Graves nodded.

"You'll be all right. Just don't inject any more of that stuff. You uncouple the tanks?"

Graves pointed.

"Well," Nordmann said. "That's it, then." He looked around the room. "Quite an elaborate setup."

With a *pluck!* Graves pulled one of the rubber suction "vibration sensors" off the wall and showed it to Nordmann.

"I'll be damned," Nordmann said. "Phony as a four-dollar bill. But he really kept us guessing."

Phelps came into the room. "What's going on here?"

"The tanks have been uncoupled," Nordmann said. "There's no danger any more."

"Good work," Phelps said. He said it to Nordmann. Graves was angry about that, but he made no gesture. There was no sense in giving Phelps the satisfaction.

Phelps left. Somebody brought Graves a glass of water. Graves sipped it and wandered around the room, looking at the equipment, touching it idly.

"Well, anyway," Nordmann said. "Congratulations."

Graves shrugged.

"You're not accepting congratulations?"

Graves finished the water, tried his voice. "I'm not sure they're in order yet."

"Why? Surely it's clear—"

"The double whammy," Graves said. "Wright is a master of it."

"That may be," Nordmann said, "but—"

"Then where's the second punch?" Graves said. He continued to wander around the room. When he came to the scintillation counter, he clicked it on. The machine chattered loudly like an angry insect.

"Damn," Nordmann said. "Everybody out!"

Graves laughed and shook his head. Everybody left the room quickly. Phelps was outside in the corridor, talking with policemen who were removing the two dead bodies. "What is it now?" Phelps asked.

"A second punch," Nordmann said. "Radiation in that room."

Phelps smiled in total triumph. "We're prepared for that," he said. He picked up a walkie-talkie. "We have a radiation hazard on the nineteenth floor," he said. "Get the shielding up here."

Graves and Nordmann exchanged glances.

"Oh," Phelps said, "I'm not a complete fool."

"Nobody ever suggested you were a *complete* fool," Nordmann said.

It took two minutes for the policeman to arrive. He entered the room with the lead cases, which were carried on small, rolling dollies. He also had a pair of long tongs. He emerged a moment later. "All clear," he said. "Two bars of some isotope. Shielded now."

Phelps smiled. "As soon as we heard about the explosive," he said, "I checked truck hijackings. There were two today: one for the explosive and another for the isotope."

"Good work," Graves said. He said it to Nordmann.

Phelps looked pained.

Graves and Nordmann went back into the room. Nordmann said, "Satisfied now?"

"Almost."

Nordmann laughed. "You're a hard man to satisfy."

"It's not me," Graves said. "It's *him*."

Nordmann looked around the room. "Well," he said, "I don't know what you expect to find here..."

"Neither do I."

"You seem so certain."

"I'm not certain. I'm just worried."

Nordmann raised an eyebrow. "A *triple* whammy?"

"Maybe."

"I think you're giving him too much credit."

"Maybe."

Graves continued to prowl around the room.

"Well," Nordmann said, "in the meantime I think we'd better move these tanks apart. Just in case. I'll be happier when they're separated by a distance of several miles."

"Okay," Graves said. He was hardly paying attention, looking at the equipment in the room. "You know," he said, "I can't get over the feeling that it's been too simple."

"Too simple? It's been complicated as hell." Nordmann put his arm over Graves's shoulder. "I think you're tired," he said gently.

Across the room Lewis said, "It's five o'clock, gentlemen." Everyone, including the cops, laughed. One or two of the men in the room clapped.

On the floor the timer wheel clicked once. There was a loud metallic snap.

The battery light blinked on.

The twin solenoids clicked to the "open" position.

And nothing happened, because the solenoids had been disengaged from the tanks.

"Well," Nordmann said, "I can't imagine that there's anything else."

"I guess not," Graves said.

He and Nordmann left the apartment and walked down the corridor toward the elevators.

San Diego: 5 p.m. PDT

Hour 0

At 5:02 Graves pressed the button for the elevator. The light didn't go on. He looked up at the floor numbers, one of which should have been lighted; they were all dark.

"That's funny," he said.

Nordmann frowned. "Maybe they went on the blink."

"Why?" Graves asked.

"Maybe when we cut the power to the apartment—"

"But they worked before."

"Yes, that's true. They did."

"Why should they break down now?"

At that moment a cop came up the stairs, panting heavily. "Damned elevators are broken down," he said. "We checked the circuit breakers in the basement. There was a timer wired in to knock out the elevators exactly at five."

"At five?" Graves asked. He looked at Nordmann.

Nordmann shrugged. "Probably just a little irritant he threw in."

"An irritant? But that doesn't make sense."

"It's plenty irritating to me," Nordmann said. "I don't want to walk down nineteen flights of stairs."

"Of course," Graves said. "But why do it now?"

"I don't get you."

"Well, if Wright wanted to make things difficult, he would have knocked out the elevators at four p.m. And that would have made things very difficult for us. It might even have delayed us until the gas went off."

"True."

"But why wait until five? By then we've either beaten his system or we haven't."

"Listen," Nordmann said, "I think you're tired. You've been worrying about Wright for so long—"

"I am not tired," Graves said, shaking off Nordmann's arm. "Wright was a logical man, and there is logic in this move."

"There are no more moves," Nordmann said. "We've won."

"Yes," Graves said. "That's exactly what we're supposed to think."

And he turned and walked back to the apartment.

"John," Nordmann said, running to catch up with him. "John, listen—"

"You listen," Graves said. "What's the point of knocking out the elevators after five?"

"It has no point. It's a foolish irritation."

"Wrong," Graves said. "It has one important point. It traps everybody on the nineteenth floor. And it traps the tanks as well."

"That's true," Nordmann said. "But it hardly matters. We've disarmed the mechanism."

"Have we?"

"Oh, for Christ's sake, of course we have. You did it yourself. You know it's disarmed."

"But what if it's not?"

"How can it not be?"

At that, Graves sighed. "I don't know," he admitted. He reentered the apartment.

HE OFTEN FEELS THAT A PROBLEM IS SOLVED
WHEN IT IS ONLY HALF FINISHED, OR TWO-
THIRDS FINISHED.

Graves remembered the psychological report as he paced the apartment, talking out loud. Nordmann watched him and listened. In the background, cops were disassembling the tank mechanisms.

"All right," Graves said. "Let's think it through. Wright designed a mechanism."

"Yes."

"And the mechanism had a purpose."

"Yes, to dump nerve gas over the city at five p.m."

Graves nodded. "And we have thwarted that."

"Yes," Nordmann said.

"Did he have any other purpose?"

"Well, I don't know. You could answer that better than anyone. Somebody mentioned something about disagreeing with the President over China—"

"No, no," Graves said. "Let's forget about motivation. Let's consider only the intent of his system. Did he intend to do anything besides dump the nerve gas?"

"Raise hell, create panic..." Nordmann shrugged.

Graves was silent, frowning at the room. "I mean," he said, "did Wright intend his elaborate mechanism to do anything besides dump the gas?"

"No," Nordmann said.

"I agree," Graves said.

There was a long pause. Graves considered everything he knew, from every angle. He could make no sense of it, but he somehow felt certain that pieces were missing. Vital pieces...

"He knew about you," Graves said suddenly.

"What?"

"He knew about you. He knew that I had called you in."

"So what?"

"Why should he care?"

"He didn't care."

Graves began to see. It was coming into focus. "Because," he said, "Wright knew about you. He knew your position, and he knew your expertise. He must have known that you could provide an antidote to the binary gas."

Nordmann said nothing.

"If he knew you could provide an antidote, then he also knew his protection—filling this room with gas—would not work. We'd break in. He knew that."

"Are you sure?"

"Yes, I'm sure. And he didn't care."

"Perhaps he was bluffing," Nordmann said.

"It's too important for a bluff. He must have had another part of his system to cover that eventuality. He must have planned it so that if we did break in, he'd still manage to win."

Nordmann considered it all very carefully. At length he sighed and shook his head. "I'm sorry, John," he said, "I think you're entirely wrong about this. You're making hypothetical sand castles in the air—"

"No!" Graves snapped his fingers. "No, I'm not. Because there was a second purpose to his system."

"What second purpose?"

"Wright was going to Jamaica, or *somewhere*, correct?"

"Correct."

"And he was not suicidal, correct?"

"Correct. He expected to get there."

"All right. Then that establishes the need for a second purpose. His mechanism had to do *two* things."

"What two things?"

"Look," Graves said. He spoke as rapidly as he could, but he was hardly able to keep pace with his racing mind. "Wright planned all this and planned it carefully. If he succeeded, a million people would die, including the President. A major political party would be wiped out. There would be national panic of incredible proportions. And for some reason, he wanted that."

"He was insane, yes…"

"But not suicidal. He planned an escape. And the question is, what about afterward?"

"Afterward?"

"Sure. Wright is on some beach sunning himself and gloating as he reads the headlines. But for how long?"

"Damn," Nordmann said, nodding.

Phelps was also listening. "I don't follow you," he said.

"You never do," Graves snapped. "But the point is this. Sooner or later, Navy men in protective suits would enter San Diego. They would determine that people died of nerve gas. They would search for the source. They would find this apartment. They would enter it. They would find the tanks. They would put the pieces together."

"And they would come after Wright," Nordmann said.

"Exactly," Graves said.

"Wherever he went, he wouldn't be safe. He would be a mass murderer and he would have left a very clear trail behind him." He gestured at all the equipment. "Would he really leave such a clear trail for others to follow?"

"It must be true," Nordmann said, getting excited. "He had to have two purposes—first to discharge the gas, and second to obliterate the evidence."

"Obliterate the evidence *how?*" Phelps asked.

Graves leaned on a tank. He turned to Nordmann. "How long would it take this cylinder of gas to discharge?"

Nordmann shrugged. "Ten or fifteen minutes." Then he said, "I see. You want to know exactly."

"Yes," Graves said.

"Why exactly?" Phelps asked.

Graves ignored him.

Nordmann said, "Normal Army pressure tanks are usually stabilized at five hundred pounds per square inch. So these tanks...Anybody got a tape measure?" He looked around the room. One of the cops had a tape. Nordmann measured the tank. "Thirty-seven inches in circumference," he said. "Eight feet long, that's ninety-six inches, with a radius of..." He wrote on a small pad, doing rapid calculations.

Phelps said to Graves, "Why do you need it exactly?"

"Because," Graves said, "Wright didn't care if we broke into this room. He had another contingency plan to cover that. And we need to know when it will take effect."

Phelps looked totally confused.

"A radius of six inches," Nordmann was saying. "And a length of ninety-six inches gives a volume...well, figure for a cylinder...at five hundred psi...let me check the nozzles..."

He wandered off. Graves said to a cop, "What time is it?"

"Five oh seven, Mr. Graves."

Nordmann finished his calculations and turned to Graves. "At normal discharge rates, it would take these tanks sixteen minutes to empty."

"That's it, then," Graves said. "At five sixteen, a bomb will go off in this room, destroying everything. We've got to find it."

Everyone paused. They stared at him.

Phelps said, "A bomb?"

"Of course. That's why he knocked out the elevators—to trap us here. In case we managed to disengage the mechanism, he wanted us here when the bomb went off, releasing the gas and eliminating the evidence."

Phelps said, "But there's no evidence of a bomb—"

"Remember the sniffer?" Nordmann asked.

Phelps frowned.

"The sniffer," Graves said, "picked up oxides of nitrogen. Plastic explosive."

"Yes…"

"Okay," Graves said. "Where is that explosive now?"

Phelps looked around the room. "I don't see it anywhere," he said.

"But the sniffer detected it."

"Yes…"

"There must be a bomb," Graves said. "And it must be in plain sight."

"Five oh eight," a cop said.

"We better get these tanks out," Nordmann said. "We don't want them damaged by the bomb."

"Right," Graves said. "And let's get the sniffer in here: It'll help us find it."

The sniffer had been taken to the other building. Phelps turned on the walkie-talkie and talked to Lewis. Lewis said he would bring it as soon as he could, but it would take time to climb nineteen flights. Phelps told him to hurry and added a string of expletives.

Meanwhile Nordmann supervised the removal of the tanks to the hallway. The cops carried them, four men to a cylinder, grunting under the weight. Graves searched the room —scanning the wall surfaces, the door, the window ledges for any irregularity, any discontinuity that would suggest the location of explosive. Plastic explosive, Compound C, could be shaped and molded into a variety of forms. That was its advantage.

It could be anywhere.

Nordmann stuck his head into the room. "Maybe you should get out of here," he said. "We can let the room blow

if the tanks are far enough away. No sense in risking anything."

"I'll stay until we find it," Graves said. He walked to the
window and looked out. He saw Lewis running across the
street with the sniffer on his shoulder.

"Five ten," Phelps said.

It would take Lewis at least two minutes to scramble up
all those stairs. Graves stared out the window, wondering
what was happening to Wright. Had they managed to cut his
body out of the wrecked car yet?

Odd, he thought, how the game continues.

"Lewis is coming," Phelps said.

"I saw."

"How much explosive is supposed to be in this room?"

"Twenty pounds."

"Christ."

Graves continued to stare out the window. Where would
Wright hide twenty pounds of explosive? What would be the
supremely logical hiding place? Nothing less would satisfy
Wright, he was sure of that.

He shifted his position at the window, careful to avoid the
jagged splinters of glass around the sill. As he did so, he
looked down at his shirt. There was printing on the shirt;
some of the lettering from the tanks had come off on his
arms and chest when he had leaned on them.

"IMEHC," it said, and then faintly, "TON OD."

He looked at his watch. 5:12.

"Where the hell is Lewis?"

Lewis appeared, running down the corridor red-faced and
out of breath. "Sorry," he said. "Came as fast as I could." He
turned on his sniffer and walked around the room, pointing
the gunlike wand, staring at the dial on the shoulder unit.

Graves and Nordmann watched him.

Lewis began with the door, then turned to the walls. He checked carefully from baseboard to ceiling. In a slow, methodical way he went entirely around the room. Finally he stopped.

5:13.

"You get a reading?"

"No," Lewis said, checking the machine. "Nothing."

"Maybe it's in another room," Nordmann said.

"I doubt it," Graves said.

"Let's check it," Lewis said. He disappeared into the bathroom, worked through it and through the adjoining bedroom of the apartment. He came back a moment later. "Maybe the machine's broken."

"How can we test it?"

"Give it a smell of some kind."

"Like what?"

"Anything strong. Cologne, perfume, food…"

Graves went to the refrigerator, but it was empty. When he came back he saw Nordmann strike a match, blow it out, and hold the smoking tip in front of the sniffer wand.

"Off the dial," Lewis said. "It works all right. Reading sulfur and carbon, minor phosphorus. It works."

"Then why isn't it picking up explosive in this room?"

Graves sighed. "Maybe I was wrong," he said. "Maybe there isn't any explosive. Maybe it's over, after all."

"There's certainly nothing in here," Lewis said.

5:14.

One of the cops came in to Nordmann. "We're going to carry the tanks down the stairs now," he said. "We—"

"Take them one at a time," Nordmann said. "I want those tanks well separated from now on."

"Okay," the cop said and went back to the hallway.

Graves stared at Lewis. "Look," he said, "there was a lot of information Wright gave us that hasn't paid off. The washing machine, the spray paint…"

As he spoke he wandered restlessly around the apartment, from the living room into the empty bedroom, then into the bathroom. He looked at himself in the bathroom mirror.

"We'll probably never know," Lewis said. "Maybe they were all false clues designed to throw us."

"And those plastic tanks," Graves said. "We've completely forgotten the fact that—"

He stopped. He stared at himself in the mirror. The lettering from the tanks that had come off on his shirt was clear now. It was reversed in the mirror.

DO NOT

CHEMI

"My God," he said. "Of course!" He went running back into the living room.

"What is it?" Nordmann said.

"What? What?"

"The tanks!" Graves said, going out to the hallway. The first tank was already being carried down the stairs. The second still lay on the hallway floor. It was the black tank, with yellow and white stenciling.

5:15.

Graves bent over the tank and rubbed the lettering. It streaked on his finger.

"Go to the window," Graves said to a cop. "Use the bullhorn and clear the street below. Do you understand? Get everybody the hell away from the street."

The cop looked confused.

"Go!"

The cop ran.

Graves pushed at the surface of the tank in front of him. His finger left a minute indentation. "That's where your plastic explosive is," he said. "It's wrapped around the tanks in thin strips—strips pressed through the rollers of an old washing machine. There must be a timer…"

He ran his fingers quickly along the surface, feeling for lumps and irregularities. He couldn't find it, but he was in a hurry.

"Christ," Lewis said, pointing his sniffer. "This is it. Plastic explosive."

"The timer, the timer…"

"It's after five fifteen," Nordmann said.

"Get those cops in the stairway away from that tank," Graves said. "Tell them to drop it and run."

His fingers raced along the surface, back and forth. But it was eight feet of tank—too much surface to cover easily. It was probably a small timer, too. Perhaps miniaturized, perhaps the size of a thumbnail.

"Damn!"

"I get it," Lewis said. "That was why he wanted inflammable plastic for the tanks. It'll explode and burn without leaving a—"

"Coming up on five sixteen," Nordmann said, looking at his watch.

Where was the timer?

"I can't find it," Graves said. "Come on." He picked up the tank by the nozzle and began dragging it back into the apartment. "Help me," he said.

There were three of them, but the 500-pound tank was bulky. As they entered the apartment, the cop at the window was on the bullhorn saying, "Clear the area, clear the area."

Graves had a quick glimpse out the window and saw that people were running. He helped lift the tank up to the sill.

"Listen," Nordmann said, "are you sure you should—"

"No choice," Graves said. "We've got to get the tanks separated."

"Five sixteen," somebody said.

They pushed the tank out the window.

The huge cylinder fell slowly, almost lazily, but picked up speed as it went. It was halfway to the street when it exploded in a violent ball of red and black flame. Graves and Nordmann, who had been looking out the window, were knocked back inside.

A moment later there was a second explosion inside the building. The walls shook. The men looked at each other. Everyone was pale.

"Jesus," Nordmann said.

"I knew it," Graves said. "We had to get that separation."

Even so, he was thinking, there might be some mixture of the gases. And just a few droplets could kill...

"We better get everybody out of here," he said. They walked back toward the stairwell. Acrid stinging smoke billowed up toward them. Graves said, "Did the cops carrying that thing get away?"

Nobody seemed to know.

The smoke coming from the stairs was so harsh that they were unable to descend. They returned to the apartment and to the windows looking down on the street. A heavy cloud of gray smoke was clearing. On the pavement there were globs of burning plastic, and smoke rising. In the distance they heard the sound of sirens and fire trucks.

Graves reached in his pocket for a cigarette, brought one out, and dropped it from his shaking hand. He took out another and lit it. He went to the window and looked down at the street. The fire trucks were coming. He watched them turn the corner and move past the police barricades.

Directly beneath him the pieces of molten plastic continued to burn on the pavement.

He turned to Nordmann. "Is he dead?"

"Who?"

"Wright."

"Yes," Nordmann said quietly. "He's dead."

Graves watched as the fire trucks pulled up and sprayed the burning plastic with long hoses. The water formed reflecting puddles, gleaming red from the firelight and the San Diego sunset. He watched the harsh, streaming water for another moment, and then turned away from the window.

"Let's go down," Nordmann said.

"Yes," Graves said. "Let's."

Epilogue:
Beta Scenario Revisions

By a complicated mechanism, John Wright, an ordinary American citizen, arranged to disperse one half-ton of ZV nerve gas over the city of San Diego at 5 P.M., August 23, 1972. This event was to coincide with the political events occurring in that city at that time.

The plan was halted by intervention of the Defense Department, with some minor assistance by State Department personnel, particularly Mr. R. Phelps.

The Department of Defense is to be congratulated on its successful efforts in this matter.

Three weeks later, the Secretary of Defense ordered a contingency study based upon reevaluation of RAND Scenario beta (theft of CBW or nuclear components).

The contingency study advised the following:

1. *Destruction of all unnecessary chemical stockpiles.* This includes all chemical agents stored aboveground (as in Rocky Mountain Arsenal, etc.). This includes all chemical agents combined with outmoded delivery systems (as in 12,000 Bolt rockets evacuated to ocean in 1969). This includes all redundant chemical agents (as in all gas GB stockpiles, now outmoded by VX, ZV).

2. *Severe limitation of transport of chemical agents.* This includes all chemical agents, in whatever quantities. The necessity for any transportation must be verified by direct order of the Secretary of Defense himself.

3. *Severe restriction of total stockpiling locations.* Chemical agents are now stored in 22 locations in the continental United States. The contingency study concluded that there was no rationale for maintaining more than 4 (±1) stockpile locations.

4. *Severe regulations governing transport of chemicals.* No quantity of chemical agent, however small, should travel with less than two platoons (80 men) who are trained to deal with subversive attempts and also with accidents during shipment.

5. *Severe regulations governing data bank access.* Classified information should be unavailable over any temporary line system. No multidrop lines should be utilized. Codings should be changed no less than every 48 hours. Permutations on each code should be no fewer than 2^5.

The report of the Beta Scenario contingency study was evaluated by the Secretary of Defense and the Joint Chiefs of Staff on November 10, 1972. The evaluation committee consisted of R. Gottlieb (RAND); K. Villadsen (Defense Systems Review); P. Lazarus (Defense C/C); L.M. Rich (State); A. Epstein (JCS); R. Dozier (Advanced Research PL); R. Phelps (State Intelligence). It was the unanimous conclusion of those present at the meeting that none of the recommendations needed to be acted on at that time. A review committee was suggested for further evaluation of the report. Members of the review committee will be appointed in the near future.

In the meantime, present regulations and operating methods remain in effect.

More Great Suspense
From the Author of
BINARY

DRUG of CHOICE

by MICHAEL CRICHTON
WRITING AS JOHN LANGE

On a secret island in the Caribbean, bioengineers have devised a vacation resort like no other, promising the ultimate
escape. But when Dr. Roger Clark investigates, he discovers
the dark secret of Eden Island and of Advance Biosystems,
the shadowy corporation underwriting it...

Read on for an excerpt
from DRUG OF CHOICE,
available now at your
favorite bookstore.

The cop, positioned at the intersection of the Santa Ana Freeway and U.S. 85, saw it all. At three in the afternoon an Angel went past him, hunched over his bike, doing a hundred and ten. The cop later remembered that the Angel had a maniacal grin on his face as he raced forward, weaving among the passenger cars.

The policeman gave chase, light flashing and siren wailing, but traffic was heavy and the Angel managed to keep his distance. He left the freeway in the foothills, and headed north into the mountains, still going more than a hundred miles an hour. The cop followed, but the bike was taking chances, and managed to pull further ahead.

After twenty minutes, the police car came around a bend and the cop saw the bike at the side of the road, lying on its side. The motor was still on, spinning the rear wheel.

The Angel lay sprawled on the ground a short distance away. He had apparently been moving slowly at the time of the accident, because he was unmarked—no cuts, no bruises, no scrapes. He was, however, comatose, and could not be roused. The policeman checked the pulse, which was strong and regular. He tried for several minutes to awaken the Angel, and then returned to his car to call an ambulance.

Roger Clark, resident in internal medicine, went on duty at the Los Angeles Memorial Hospital at six. When he arrived on the floor, he went to see Baker, the day resident. Baker was in the dressing room, changing from his whites to street clothes. He looked tired.

"How're things?" Clark said, stripping off his sportcoat and putting on a white jacket.

"Okay. Not much excitement, except for Mrs. Leaver. She still pulls out her intravenous lines when she thinks nobody's looking."

Clark nodded, stepping to the mirror and straightening his tie.

"And then Henry," Baker said. "He had the DT's this morning, and sat in the corner arguing with the little green men."

"How is he now?"

"We gave him some librium, but watch him. One of the nurses said he felt her up last night."

"Who's that?"

"Alice."

"Alice? He must really be hallucinating if he felt her up."

"Well, just don't mention it to Alice. She's very sensitive."

Baker finished dressing, lit a cigarette, and rapidly went through the status of the other patients. Nothing much had changed since Clark had gone off duty twenty-four hours before.

"Oh," Baker said. "Almost forgot a new admission. One of those Hell's Angels. The cops brought him in after he had a motorcycle accident. He was comatose and he hasn't come out yet."

"You ask for a neurological consult?"

"Yeah, but they probably won't get around to it until morning."

"What's his status now?"

"We did the usual stuff. Skull films negative, CSF normal, chest films okay, EEG vaguely abnormal, but nothing specific. All his reflexes are there."

"Cardiorespiratory depression?"

"Nope. He's just fine. To look at him, you'd think he was asleep."

"You treating?"

"No, we're waiting for the consult. Let the neuro boys play around with him for a while."

"Okay. Anything else?"

"No. That's it." Baker smiled. "See you tomorrow."

When he was alone, Clark made a quick round of the wards, checking on the patients. Everyone seemed in pretty good shape. When he came to the comatose Angel, he paused.

The patient was young, in his early twenties. Nobody had washed him since admission; his hair was greasy, his face was unshaven and streaked with grit, and his fingernails were rimmed with black. He lay quietly in bed, not moving, breathing slowly and easily. Clark checked him over, listening to the heart, tapping out the reflexes. He could find nothing wrong. They had put an intravenous line into him, and had catheterized him in case of urinary retention. The catheter tube led to a bottle on the floor. He looked at it.

The urine was bright blue.

Frowning, he held the bottle up to the light and looked closely. It was an odd, vivid blue, almost fluorescent.

What turned urine blue?

He went back to the desk, hoping to catch Baker and ask about the urine, but Baker was gone. Sandra, the night nurse, was there.

"Were you on duty when they brought that Angel in?"

"Arthur Lewis? Yes."

"What happened?"

Sandra shrugged. "The police brought him into the emergency ward. They figured he'd had an accident, so they took him up to X-ray and checked him over. No broken bones, nothing. All the enzymes and electrolytes came back normal. The EW couldn't figure it out, so they shipped him up here. It's all very mysterious. He was going a hundred before the accident, but the police think he slowed way down before it happened. The policeman who found him said it was just as if he had suddenly fallen asleep."

"Ummm," Clark said. He bit his lip. "What about his urine?"

"What about it?"

"Has it always been blue?"

Sandra frowned and left the desk. She went into the ward and looked at the bottle, then returned. "I've never seen anything like that," she said.

"Neither have I."

"What turns urine blue?"

"I was just wondering the same thing," Clark said. "Why don't you call down to neurology and say the guy is still in a coma, but urinating blue. Maybe that'll bring them up."

Ten minutes later, Harley Spence, Chief of Neurology, appeared on the seventh floor, panting slightly. He was a white-haired man in his middle fifties, very proper in a three-piece suit.

His first words to Clark were: "Urinating blue?"

"That's right, sir."

"How long has this been going on?"

"Apparently it just started, within the last few minutes."

"Fascinating," Spence said. "Perhaps a new kind of porphyria. Or some idiosyncratic drug reaction. Whatever it is, it's definitely reportable."

Clark nodded. In his mind, he saw the journal article:

"H.A. Spence: Unusual Urinary Pigment in a Comatose Man. Report of a Case."

They walked to the patient's bed. Clark ran through the story while Spence began his examination. Arthur Lewis, twenty-four, unemployed, first admission through the EW in a coma after a motorcycle accident...

"Motorcycle accident?" Spence said.

"Apparently."

"He's unmarked. Not a scratch on him. Would you say that's likely?"

"No sir, but that's the police story."

"Ummm."

Muttering to himself, Spence conducted his neurological examination. He worked briskly at first, and then more slowly. Finally he scratched his head.

"Remarkable," he said. "Quite remarkable. And this urine —bright blue."

Spence stared at the bottle, hesitated, then turned to Clark. "What makes urine blue?"

Clark shrugged.

Spence shook his head, put the bottle down. He stepped back from the patient and looked at him.

"Jesus Christ, blue piss," he said. "What a patient."

And he walked off.

The metabolic boys came around an hour later; they collected several samples for analysis, amid a lot of vague talk about tubular secretory rates and refractile indices; Clark listened to them until he was sure they had no idea what was going on. Then, as he was leaving, one of them said, "Listen, Rog, what do you make of this?"

"I don't make anything of it," Clark said.

"Do you think it's a drug thing? You're the local expert."

Clark smiled. "Hardly." He had done two years of drug testing at Bethesda, but it had been boring work, measuring excretion and metabolism of experimental drugs in animals and, occasionally, in human subjects. He had only done it because it got him out of the army.

"Well, could it be a bizarre drug reaction?"

Clark shrugged. "It could. Of course it could. Even a common drug like aspirin can produce strange reactions in certain people."

Someone else said, "What about an entirely new drug?"

"Like what?"

"I don't know. But these Angels will take anything in a capsule. Remember the guy we got who had swallowed a hundred birth control pills?"

"I don't think that birth control pills would turn—"

"No, no, of course not. But what if this is some entirely new drug, some new thing like STP or THC or ASD?"

"Possible," Clark said. "Anything's possible." On that note, the metabolic boys went back to the labs, clutching their urine samples, and Clark went back to work.

Word of the Angel quickly spread through the hospital. A constant stream of doctors, residents, interns, students, nurses, and orderlies appeared on the floor to look at Arthur Lewis and his urine bottle. During all this time, the patient continued to sleep peacefully. Repeated attempts to rouse him by calling his name, shaking him, or pinching him were unsuccessful.

At midnight, everything on the floor seemed quiet, and Clark went to bed. He stretched out on the cot in the resident's room, fully dressed, and fell asleep almost immediately.

At five in the morning, he got a call from Sandra. She needed him on the seventh floor; she couldn't say more. She sounded frightened, so he went right up.

When he arrived, he found Sandra talking to an immense, bearded man in black leather. Though all the lights on the floor had been turned off except the nightlights, the man wore sunglasses. He had a huge naked angel painted on the back of his leather jacket, and on his hand was a tattoo of a heart pierced by an arrow. Underneath, in gold lettering, it said "Twat."

Clark walked up to him. "I'm Dr. Clark. Can I help you?"

Sandra gave a sigh of relief and sat down. The Angel turned to Clark, looked him up and down. He was a head taller than Clark.

"Yeah, man. You can help me."

"How?"

"You can let me see Artie-baby."

"I'm afraid that's not possible."

"Come on, not possible. What is this not possible shit? You sound like a doctor."

"I am a doctor."

"Then you can let me see Artie-baby. All the time, this one keeps saying she can't let me see him because she's not a doctor. So okay, I buy it, right? It's a slide, but I buy it. Now you start in. What is this?"

"Look," Clark said, "it's five in the morning. Visiting hours don't begin until—"

"Visiting hours are for creeps, man."

"I'm sorry. We have certain rules here."

"Yeah, but you know what happens if I come visiting hours? I see all the sickies, and it makes me depressed, you know? It's a down, a real bummer. But now it's dark."

"That's true."

"Yeah, so okay. Right?"

"I'm sorry. Your friend is in a coma now. You can't see him."

"Little Jesus? In a coma? Naw: he wouldn't do a thing like that."

Clark said, "Little Jesus?"

"That's his name, man. He had the crucifixion thing, you know. Every trip, he wants to get nailed. His bag: too much money, he had an unhappy childhood."

Not knowing what else to say, Clark said, "You'd better go now. Come back in the morning."

"I'll be flying by then, man. Soon as I leave, I'm flying."

Clark paused. "Does your friend also fly?"

"Sure, man. All the time. He doesn't like his momma, see, so he does a lot of flying. He saw a shrink, too, but that wasn't as good as a long flight."

"What was he flying?"

"You name it. Dope, Gold, Mishra, glue, acid when he was up to it, B's all the time, goofies…"

"Did he ever try anything really unusual?"

The Angel frowned. "You got a line on something?"

"No," Clark said. "Just wondered."

"Naw, he was pretty straight. Never shot stuff, even. He's the oral type, you know." The Angel paused. "Now how about it. Do I see him, or what?"

Clark shook his head. "He's in a coma."

"You keep talking this coma crap."

There was a moment of silence, and the Angel reached into his pocket. Clark heard a metallic click as the switch-blade snapped open. The knife glinted in the light.

"I don't want to call the police," Clark said.

"I don't want to carve your guts out. Now lead the way. I just wanna see him, and then I'll leave. Right?"

Clark felt the tip against his stomach. He nodded.

They went into the ward. The Angel stood at the foot of the bed and watched Arthur Lewis for several minutes. Then he reached into his pocket, fumbled, and frowned. He whispered, "Shit. I forgot it."

"Forgot what?"

"Nothing. Shit."

They went back outside.

"Were you bringing him something?" Clark asked.

"No, man. Forget it, huh?"

The Angel stepped to the elevator. Clark watched him as he got in.

"One last thing," the Angel said. "Cool it with the security guards, or we'll have blood in the lobby."

Clark said cheerfully, "You can see him tomorrow, if you like. Visiting hours from two to three thirty."

"Man, he won't be here that long."

"His coma is quite deep."

"Man, don't you understand? He isn't in no coma."

The doors closed, and the elevator descended.

"I'll be damned," Clark said, to no one in particular. He went back to bed.

Visit rounds began at ten. The visit today was Dr. Jackson, a senior staff member of the hospital. Clark disliked Jackson, and always had. The feeling was mutual.

Jackson was a tall man with short black hair and a sardonic manner. He made little cracks as he accompanied Clark and the interns around from patient to patient. Late in the morning, they came to Arthur Lewis. Clark presented the case, summarizing the now-familiar story of the motorcycle accident, and the police, the admission through the emergency ward...

Jackson interrupted him before he finished. "That man isn't comatose. He's asleep."

"I don't think so, sir."

"You mean to tell me," Jackson said, "that that son-of-a-bitch lying there is in a coma?"

"Yes, sir. The chief of neurology, Dr. Spence, thought so too. He saw the patient—"

"Spence is an old fart. Step aside." He pushed past the interns and stepped to the head of the bed. He peered closely at Lewis, then turned to Clark.

"Watch closely, doctor. This is how you wake a sleeping patient."

Clark suppressed a smile, and managed a solemn nod.

Jackson bent over Arthur Lewis.

"Mr. Lewis, Mr. Lewis."

The patient did not stir.

"Wake up, Mr. Lewis."

No reaction.

Jackson shook the patient's head gently, then with increasing force. There was no response.

"Mr. Lew-is. Time to get up…"

He continued this for several moments, and then, suddenly, slapped Arthur Lewis soundly across the face.

Clark stepped forward. "Sir, I don't think—"

At that moment, Arthur Lewis blinked his eyes, opened them, and smiled.

Jackson stepped back from the bed with a grin of triumph. "Exactly, Dr. Clark. You don't think. This man is simply a heavy sleeper, difficult to rouse. My youngest son is the same way."

He turned to the patient. "How do you feel?"

"Great," Arthur Lewis said.

"Have a good sleep?"

"Yeah, great." He sat up. "Where am I?"

"You're in the L.A. Memorial Hospital, where the resident staff believes that there is something wrong with you."

"Me? Wrong with me? I feel great."

"I'm sure you do," Jackson said, with a quick glance at Clark. "Would you mind walking around for us?"

"Sure, man." The Angel started to get up, then stopped. He felt under the sheets. "Hey, what's going on here? Somebody's been fooling with my—"

At that moment, for the first time, Clark remembered the blue urine. He moved around to the side of the bed and picked up the bottle. "By the way, Dr. Jackson," he said, "there is one unsolved question here. This man's urine. It's blue."

Clark held up the bottle.

"It is?" Jackson said, frowning.

Clark looked at the bottle. The urine was yellow.

"Well," he said lamely, "it was."

"Isn't that interesting," Jackson said, with a pitying smile.

"Hey, listen," the Angel said. "Get this damned tube outa me. It feels funny. What kinda pervert did a thing like that, anyhow?"

Jackson rested a reassuring hand on the patient's shoulder. "We'll take care of it right away. Just lie back for a minute. As long as you're here, you might as well have lunch with the other patients."

The rounds group moved off to the next case. The interns were muttering among themselves. Clark stared at the floor.

"I swear to you, sir. Last night his urine was bright blue. I saw it; Dr. Spence saw it; the metabolic boys saw—"

"At this moment," said Dr. Jackson, "I am perfectly willing to believe that you saw polka-dot urine. In this hospital, anything is possible."

The patient, Arthur Lewis, was discharged at 1:00 P.M. Before he left, Clark talked with him. The patient remembered nothing about a motorcycle accident, or the police. He claimed he had been sitting in his room, smoking a cigarette, when he fell asleep. He awoke in the hospital; he remembered nothing in between. When Clark asked if he had ever urinated blue before, the Angel gave him a funny look, laughed, and walked away.

There were jokes about Clark at lunch that day, and for several weeks afterward. But eventually it blew over, and was forgotten. For Clark, there was only one really disturbing aspect to the whole situation.

The day Arthur Lewis was discharged, Clark had stopped at the front desk on his way home, and talked to the lobby staff.

"I hope there wasn't any trouble about that Angel in here last night," he said.

"Oh, he was discharged this morning," a receptionist said.

"No, I mean his friend. A huge guy. Came up to the seventh floor at five a.m. with a switchblade."

"Friend?"

"Yes. Another Angel."

"At five in the morning?" the receptionist said.

"Yes."

"I was on duty all night. There was no Angel. I do remember an awfully big man—"

"That's him. Very big man."

"—but he was wearing a sportcoat and turtleneck. And he had a little briefcase. Very pleasant-looking man."

Clark frowned. "You're sure?"

The receptionist smiled in a friendly way. "Quite sure, Dr. Clark."

"Well, that's very peculiar."

"Yes," she said, with a slow nod. "It is."